SOMETIMES I WRITE THINGS DOWN

Short Stories, Tales and Anecdotes

Fiction, Facts and Lies

Oliver Stack

First published in 2020 by Paragon Publishing, Rothersthorpe

© Oliver Stack 2020

Cover Photo: **Oaklawn Sunrise** *Oliver Stack*
Back Cover Photo: **Shreelawn Sunset** *Oliver Stack*

ISBN 978-1-78222-787-8

Book design, layout and production management by Into Print
www.intoprint.net
+44 (0)1604 832149

Dedicated to my Parents

Acknowledgments

Anything I ever thought might be worth doing, has always proved to be far more difficult than I at first anticipated. No less so, is the book you are holding. It most certainly would never have happened, but for those few people that showed me the way. They'd read some pieces I'd written, liked what I did, and asked for more.

Every line on every page is dedicated to all those wonderful people (and there were many) who picked me up when I fell, and had belief in me, when I'd so little faith in myself.

Who are they? I don't have to give names; they'll know who I mean. Geographically they're spread far and wide and I owe them all a huge debt of gratitude. There's no currency on earth that can repay it, so for what it's worth, this is just my way of showing my appreciation, and saying thanks.

Oliver Stack

CONTENTS

The Day a Mountain Stole my Soul

'Today boys, we just might be going hillwalking'

The time was in mid-April. A fine spring morning that carried the promise of summer. That day, as is usual, I went to walk my two companions, *Twister and Buddy*. There I was, in the best of company, and what a beautiful day to be blessed with. A morning to be remembered; could life get any better? It was the morning that a mountain stole my soul.

At the crossroads on the western end of the village, I sat gazing out to the magnificent vista of the East Limerick landscape. I could see my mountain in the distance. I got an urge, which was quite unexplainable, to throw caution aside and travel further than normal.

I've no problem in passing the time of day with my dogs. Sometimes, in fact I'm sure, they have a better understanding of the spoken word than most of us so-called intelligent people. They know and understand me. I try and do the same with them. 'Today boys,' says I, 'we just might be going hill-walking.'

A look passed between them. I know that look so well. Twister nudged Buddy. The look clearly said, 'De boss has totally lost it.' Once more I gazed out on my beloved Bally-houras, and went for it.

Unprepared? Foolhardy and stupid?

Yes. Undoubtedly so.

Equipped for adventures or the unforeseen?

No. I most certainly was not.

Not even the basics. No high-viz vest, no rough terrain boots and only God or the Devil would have any inkling of my whereabouts. The night before I'd left my phone in a safe place, but thanks to the intervention of a senior moment, I couldn't remember where.

No doubt an experienced hill-walker would have berated me with some well-intentioned advice, before packing me off home with the outline of a bootsole imprinted on my rump. Using the vernacular of the region, he'd have busted my hole.

On the positive side, what I did have, was a beautiful morning and enthusiasm for adventure. Faster than a thirsty bullock scenting water, we travelled out the Ardpatrick road. We rattled past the Cross of Red Chair, going like the clappers until we reached the foot of Seefin mountain. There, in the tiny village of Glenosheen, we commenced our adventure.

As solid today as when they were built (in or about 1710), two very attractive stone-built houses stand just by the junction of the road. Here is where some of the Palatine people from Germany settled more than three centuries ago. Beside being expert cattle breeders, they made an outstanding success of growing hemp and flax.

From there, with the exuberance of children, we wended our way skywards, towards that distant summit. On a morning I thought could get no better, it did.

The sun obliged. Through pencil-thin cracks in cotton-wool clouds rays of golden light streaked earthwards. Water, after recent rainfalls, cascaded down from the heights. Gurgling and murmuring, it sparkled like newly-polished silver, as it rolled down that stony pathway. Underfoot, the rough stone track had all the characteristics of a stream bed, as it crawled in a higgledy-piggledy line, towards summit of the majestic Seefin.

Water with the temperture of ice filled my boots. Did I mind? Good Lord No! Why would I? It took me back to my childhood, a lot of which was spent in this same countryside.

I marvelled at the magnificence of the landscape. The black, whites and browns of a variety of cattle, foraged for grass between ferns, heather and gorse. Suckling calves bawled. Somewhere below me, a bull bellowed.

The first swallows of the spring flitted about. They flew high above Glenosheen against the backdrop of that beautiful blue sky, as they checked for the nesting places of the previous year. The dogs investigated rabbit holes, before following the trails left by the wanderings of nocturnal hunters. Happily mud-spattered, they splashed on regardless. The only intrusion to the silence were the twittering of bird-song and the gurgling of water. The higher the path took us the more silent it became.

That day it was brought home to me, and not for the first time, how privileged I am to live in such an inspiringly beautiful countryside. The views here are like no place else, they truly are to die for. In this place the tall pines kiss the sky, and clouds make love to the mountains.

The air is pure. Breathe deeply and you're surely imbibing the scent of Heaven.

Beneath me, set against rich green woodland, the village of Ballyorgan clung like a suckling child to the breast of a distant hillside. Farmhouses and cottages lay scattered across the landscape. A landscape, that in the sunlight, was like an ornate piece of patchwork quilting, blessed with every shade of green imaginable.

From my vantage point, I looked down on the magnificent building that is Castle Oliver. It was from there that the stunningly beautiful adventuress Lola Montez first looked out on this magical landscape. Here in the rural Ballyhoura countryside is where that lady's escapades began. She went on to find fame as a dancer, courtesan and mistress of one Ludwig 1st of Bavaria, who bestowed on her the title of Countess.

On some fine day in summer, I promised myself, I would return and reach the summit of that mountain. It's not the hightest there is, but who cares? It'll do for me.

I can well imagine being in that same spot on a warm summer's night, and hanging the cares of the day from the horns of a crescent moon. Since I came to live here, this place has captured me, heart and soul. I wouldn't want it any other way. I can dream here. Nobody will invade my space, or alter the course of my dreams.

I did go back. On an equally beautiful day, I climbed that pathway again. Three-quarters way up, I was sitting on a rock, taking a break, when two fit looking ladies came up the pathway. By fit, I mean they weren't like me, struggling for breath. They stopped to chat. Nice ladies, mother and daughter. After a few minutes, they tootled on up towards the summit. Me? I gave serious consideration to lying down flat, and rolling all the way to the bottom. That's when I imagined I heard the crack and felt the lash of the Devil's riding crop. I couldn't let two ladies best me. I had to carry on. Stubborn as a mule, I set off in pursuit.

Good job my dog Twister has the muscles of a buffalo,

and is every bit as strong. He took the strain and pulled me in the right direction. Fifty yards on the situation changed completely. In that the pathway became almost vertical, and was probably akin to taking a hike on the dark side of the Moon. Rough? It wasn't in it.

The distance between myself and the ladies in front, widened appreciably. *'Slow down you eejit, it's not a race,'* gasped I to myself. I knew if I didn't my blood pressure would reach the top a lot sooner than I would. With the sweat coming off me in buckets, I eventually crawled on to summit.

The two ladies were sharing a thermos of coffee and some scones. The younger woman rummaged in her bag and very kindly offered me a bottle of spring water. I wasn't slow about accepting it. I think she might just have saved my life. Again, we struck up a conversation. It was a very sad, and touching story, they'd to tell.

They'd travelled over from Dromcollagher in County Limerick. I'd nothing against them being from Limerick. I have cousins that live in that same county. The mother, God love her, had breast cancer. When all the chemotherapy sessions were over, she'd made herself a bucket list. On that list, was her wish to climb a mountain. She wanted to see what she could from, what she thought of, as the top of the world. Seefin mountain was her choice. She lived some thirty miles away in a westerly direction, and on a clear day, she could always see the mountain top.

Lovely people, brave people. Coming to terms with, and coping as best they could, with what the vagaries of life had thrown at them. I sat in for a photo, before watching them depart. I thought that old saying very true. *'Strangers are really friends, you've just met for the first time.'*

I sat on that mountain top for an hour after they'd gone. That woman was a far stronger person than I could ever hope to be. Thankful for what little I had, I realised I was blessed. It's a good feeling. Believe me, there is no feeling on earth quite like it.

On the downhill trek, Buddy picked his way carefully from rock to rock. Twister shot down that mountainside on his haunches, with me trying to hold tight to whatever piece of nothing, my life was still worth.

Before leaving, I looked back to where I'd been. I know now, that this is as close, to that place called Heaven as I am ever likely to get. Someday when I cross to the other side, I won't be looking for a supposedly better place. You see, I found it, a very long time ago.

A Walk on the Wet Side
(I Hate Election Posters)

Sunday. The first one in Feburary 2016. The first Sunday of Spring. Another morning when the sky fell on the mountains and clouds tumbled to earth. In the way of rain clouds, they fell two at once, slobbering big wet kisses on an already waterlogged landscape. Me? Rain-soaked and wet, my dogs and I squelched our way happily onwards. The breath-taking beauty of my beloved Bally-houras is, for me, a sight that always lifts my spirits. I love it here. This place is my home. That's why I hate so much to see it defaced. It hurts me.

This morning every post, pole or tree that could be utilised was adorned by a mugshot of a wannabe politician.

My word! Don't they look good? Maybe … Perhaps… In the eyes of their mothers, or the rose-tinted vision of their nearest and dearest. Me? No! Definitely not.

The oversized images of these made-up, air-brushed clowns, beaming insincerity, are a blight on the splendour of the countryside.

The village of Kildorrery is, without doubt, a jewel on this stretch of the Ballyhoura mountains. To see it defiled by the sweet as treacle, toothpaste white smiles on the posters of opportunists offends me. This is, for want of a better word, what I would term as legalised graffiti. When the race is run and the last (mislaid) ballot box has finally surfaced, will these same smirking, fly-by-night chancers remove them as quickly? Some will, some won't. Despite there being (miracle of miracles) legislation for that sort of thing, but their are always the cowboys that think that rules are for other people. Then this is Ireland, so what can one expect? Rules only apply to those who wish to abide by them.

Suddenly, right there, in my little corner of heaven, I saw a crack in the gloomy façade. A little light seeped in. With the swiftness of a laser it crumbled my despair. Faith was restored. There is a bright side. It might well be the last time I'll see many of them hanged.

The Changing of the Guard

She observed their progress; in truth, she despised them all

L izzie O'Mahony stirred, rolled over on the too-narrow pallet bed, and listened. It was the wind that had woken her. It screamed a little louder and with a sharp crack a branch snapped from a tree somewhere on the lane. She dragged herself off the mattress and staggered sleepily to the edge of her child's cot. The child was her pride and joy. She was her first-born, and though just over half-a-year old, she already had the same dark, crow-black hair as her father. Curly and thick, it rolled almost to her shoulders. She settled the cot blanket snuggly about him, before marking her forehead with the sign of the cross. *'Such a good child,'* she thought, as she slipped back to the warmth beside her sleeping husband. The wind seemed fiercer. *Let it blow. She'd be married come Easter time to a good man. Her baby would have a proper father then. What more could she ask for? She was blessed. Truly blessed.'* Her eyes closed, and she drifted back, deep into the realms of sleep.

Hissing and spitting, in the brevity of a heartbeat, the rat arched its back once. It was all the time left it, before a final screech sucked the life from its grey-clad bones. That sound would echo for eternity on the winds that swirled across the bog-land. In the space of that same heartbeat its air-borne body landed with a dull thump on the cracked ivy-covered lid of an old limestone burial vault. Death was as instantaneous as it was unexpected. That painfilled sound in the final moment of terror conveyed its life history to any that were listening. Tonight, on Halloween, there was no one.

A cat, that a moment before had been crawling through the decaying ivy, froze into immobility. Even predators knew when to feel fear. The only sound was the almost muted whistling of the wind through the branches of some ancient yew trees.

At the base of an old elm, where the shadows were deepest, the nemesis of the misfortunate rat made no movement. She listened. Her vaporizing breath rose slowly in the frost laden air. At last it came, a sound that grew louder with every passing second, but posed no threat to her.

Watching, as the train drew nearer to where the trees were tallest, she waited for the clatter of steel wheels on iron rails to mask any sound she might inadvertently make. It was merely a precaution. Making mistakes wasn't on her agenda.

There were those, if they'd known her, who would have deemed her as a witch. Witch? Just a name people who knew no better, bestowed on a woman whose intelligence was beyond their comprehension.

Others would have said insane. Insane? Who did know her? Nobody. Had she wished she could have told them a time had been when Gods had fought for her favours. They'd heard rumours, but down through the ages only a few had ever looked upon her countenance, they, the chosen ones, were truly insane.

Suddenly, the silence of the night was shattered by white-wall noise of the trains booming bass horn. She didn't flinch. Taking advantage of the noise, the cat escaped to the shelter afforded by a long-abandoned rabbit hole.

East to West, the train came fast and went by faster. Passengers, most pretending levity, chatted and laughed, boring each other silly with the stories of their day. Some read. Others struggled with the evening paper crossword. Some played cards. Some eyeing each other from behind the pages of a variety of glossy magazines, made mental promises to book appointments with hair salons and nail bars. A few, quite a few, thought a visit to an off-licence could fix a hell of a lot of hair and nails. After all, if beauty wasn't in the eye of the beholder; what was?

Young women, all blonde-haired clones of each other, fiddled with phones. They giggled inanely as fingernails like multi-coloured talons, tapped text buttons in a frenzy. Transmitting the mundane. Stuff they considered of such importance, that life itself was balanced on what they might impart to a waiting world. That was the stiletto shod, stick-thin, model of the species. The fat ones were the same. The added ingredient being multiple pounds of obese flesh, hanging over the tops of too tight trousers.

A young mother struggled to cope with the wayward antics of two over-tired children. On the seat opposite, her husband, totally oblivious to her predicament, was doing his best peacock impression. The fat fool was preening himself; for the attention of flighty looking woman old enough to know better. Ooh! It was game on. No guessing that.

Every now and then she glanced at him, seductively running the tip of her tongue across her mauve glossed lips, leaving fat boy the impression he was in with a chance. Ever so slowly she parted her thighs, allowing him a fleeting glimpse of pale flesh above black stocking tops. His eyes glazed over. She wasn't? Was she? Surely not...?

For an instant the train lights flickered; it was game over. Fat-boy, all but comatose at what he imagined he might have seen, failed to see her smirk before moving to a seat further down the carriage. He also failed to see, glistening on the cheeks of his pretty young wife, the despair that had trickled from her eyes.

There were those that slept. Dreaming dreams filled with golden hopes for days that might never materialise and would never seem as good again.

The one factor common to all was how ignorant of their unimportance they were. Ignorant of how close their demise would be if the watcher so wished.

The train lights faded into nothingness. With a final faraway blast on the bass horn, it was gone. Oh, how she despised them. Humans! How she hated that word.

Pulling her ankle-length cloak more tightly about her wraith-thin form, she began to move. Quietly, ever so quietly, she moved without sound. The thick carpet of autumn leaves on the pathway did not rustle underfoot as she passed. Though a keen observer might be forgiven for thinking that they cringed aside at her approach.

Ancient gravestones sprouted from the long, withered grass with no deference to symmetry or regularity. On the vault, where the already frozen corpse of the rat lay, the silver moonlight reflected off its fangs. Its last snarl, now set firmly in the grimace of death, gave it the appearance of smiling in agreement with whatever thoughts its executioner may have had.

She had thoughts. Two. The first one was that she hated rats. The other was that she didn't hate them quite as much as she hated humans. Loathsome creatures. She had yet to see a purpose for them, and if there was, she had never seen it to be any good. They were the enemy. Everything on earth that had once been beautiful, they'd set about destroying.

From far back in a memory as old as time she'd remembered hearing that God (he who called himself the one true God) had made man in his own likeness. What sort of God could bestow a legacy like that upon the earth? If it was the best he could do, how could it all have gone so badly wrong?

However, the shortcomings of the species were not within the parameters of her mandate. She had a task to complete and questioning it was unthinkable. Satisfied, she cackled. A sound not unlike an angry gander.

During the long balmy evenings, about the time of the last summer solstice, she'd pass this way. She'd noticed then, that even in time of fine weather, people avoided the proximity of the bog-lands. Though not so much as the old graveyard with tumbled down tower of the ancient abbey, still pointing like a sentinel at the sky.

On a night like tonight, Halloween, they crossed themselves and took to the backroads as if the cemetery was something to be feared. Humans! *Pah!* She spat. They went in dread where there was nothing to fear but fear itself. Baring discoloured teeth, she smiled as she thought of how these ignorant peasants clung to their stupid superstitions.

The night was cold. Not one for leaving the comfort of the hearthside to wander where who knew what might be lying in wait. Earlier she had passed some cottages, thatched roofs and whitewashed walls. Firewood and turf stacked neatly against the gables were already covered by the first white frost of winter. Smoke drifted from chimney tops bringing the heady aroma of turf and pinewood to scent the chill night air.

She'd peered through tiny windowpanes as parents played snap-apple, pin-the-tail-on-the-donkey and other Halloween night games with cherub-cheeked kids. Fathers laughed uproariously as children giggled. Mothers, a few with a baby on the breast, stoked the fires to keep the big black kettles boiling.

They thought they were happy. *Huh! The fools were so happy they made her sick. Idiots! Couldn't they understand that the sound of laughter was nauseous. How could they laugh amidst the destruction they were wreaking?*

She had no sympathy for their plight. Soon, very soon, there would be new blood, new order and a new beginning. They'd be held to account. The day of judgement was fast approaching.

She passed *'The Flying Angels'* public house. More stupidity. Angels hadn't flown in a millennium or more. They never would again. She'd see to that.

An out-of-tune singer was accompanied by the music of a concertina. From high on a gargoyle of the near-collapsed tower, an owl watched her approach. Hooting twice, it shed some feathers, as wings fluttering, he flew south across the bogs, erasing her from his memory.

Soon she stood before the remains of what had once been an old monastery. Heavy oak doors that had once guarded the arched entrance, were long gone. All that re-mained was a single rusted iron hinge hanging from the moss-covered stones. From time immemorial, farm animals had used it as protection, to shelter from the biting cold of winter. Tonight, as if a sixth sense warned them of something unknown, they'd stayed away.

She passed beneath the carved stone lintel and stepped on to the rough-hewn limestone flags that in another time had borne the footsteps of peasants and kings. From a cloak pocket she produced the stub of a greasy candle and flint. A flicker and moments later, through eyes of the deepest Prussian Blue, she surveyed her surroundings.

They were all here, but she expected no less. All those that had ever passed beneath the portals or officiated before the altar were here. Holy men and monks, those that had guarded the secret for centuries, stood before her. To a man they had died, that tonight she might stand here.

She had no fear. Ignoring the ghosts that walked beside her, she searched for signs. Scraping the animal droppings aside with the heels of her high-buttoned boots, she saw the marks etched deeply in the floor. A prophecy laid down, when man had evolved into little more than a cave-dweller, was about to be fulfilled.

On her knees, she rubbed at the stones until blood showed through the skin. Then with a piece of broken slate, she drew in the connecting points between the marks. A perfect pentangle. The lighting candle stub she placed between the centre of the marks; soon it would be time.

As the moon progressed across the night sky, she squatted back on her haunches, and watched its progress. A billion light years away, a star in a distant constellation, lined with the horns of the crescent moon. On the ground before her the moonlight created a perfect arc across the top points of the pentangle.

Standing, she allowed the cloak to fall from her shoulders. Like black puddle, it lay on the ground at her feet. Beneath it she was naked. Near translucent white hair hung loosely to her waist.

The woman raised her arms high, then in a language long forgotten, she began to chant an incantation in a voice that belied her appearance. It was strong, pure and sweet. Frost formed on the aureoles surrounding her nipples and on the sparse thatch of her pubic hair. She was impervious to the cold.

The rising and falling cadence of the chant went on and on. Her arms dropped. Across the inside of her left hand, just above the wrist, was a branding of an inverted cross. For a second it seemed to glow as the last of the moonlight caught its outline, then it faded from sight. The chanting dropped to a whisper, then stopped.

Suddenly, from out of nowhere, the wind changed to gale-force. It screamed across the open countryside and entered the ruins with the power of a hurricane. Picking up the cloak from the floor, it tossed the heavy garment high into the air. Shredded to rags, it vanished in the darkness. Of the woman there was no sign. The marks on the floor had disappeared.

The winds dropped as suddenly as they'd risen. The normal noises of the night returned. Far above the floor, the owl returned to its perch on the gargoyle. Vermin scurried across the floor. Seeking sanctuary from the frost, some cows and two large Clydesdales entered. One of the horses foraged among some discarded fodder.

Dawn broke slowly. From a nearby farm a cock heralded a new day. A dog barked, as it fetched the cows for milking. Wisps of fog drifted lazily across the frost covered bog. It was another normal morning.

The early risers stirred, reluctantly. Men stamped about in heavy boots, grumbling about the cold. Women rubbed sleep from their eyes, while trying to coax life back into still warm ashes.

Lizzie O'Mahony set the fire. 'One egg or two?' she asked her husband. 'Ah now stop.' Laughingly, she slapped away his wandering hands. 'Enough of that now boyo. Work won't wait. Ye know full well that my little honey pot will still be here when you get home. Now, get yer hands off me arse, yer mind off me fanny, and go earn us a crust.'

Those were the last coherent words her husband ever heard from her.

Climbing the stairs to the half-loft to check on her first born, she again blessed her good fortune. Then smiling, she looked as her gurgling baby raised its arms, as if in adoration.

Lizzie O'Mahony looked into the dark depths of her baby's blue eyes. She saw the world as it was, how it once had been and what it could yet become. Her screams shattered the quietness of the morning. In the space of a single heartbeat, her mind deserted her forever.

It brought half-dressed, panic-stricken neighbours running from their homes. The screams carried to the edge of the village and across the bog. From the wetlands, shrieking birds took flight. Household pets cowered in terror. Dogs chased their tails and cats hid in trees.

The palms of the infant were torn and bleeding. The brand of the inverted cross was clearly visible on her left hand.

The time had come. The new order had begun.

A Photo-Finish

Somewhere up there, was a God

Crackling with static the mistuned radio, belonging to one Samwell Barr, spat and hissed as it spewed out the lyrics of the one song Sammy, (everybody called him that) had no wish to hear. Not in the run-up to Christmas or any other time. Why had it ever been written? Images of broken teeth, wasted years, decades of hard living and neglect, came to mind before the singer warbled a note. So much time. All wasted in a haze of cigarette smoke and excesses of alcohol. For most of his useless life he'd staggered along that road. A few (quite a few) times he'd fallen. He'd gotten back up, but he wasn't proud of what he'd left behind. It was no place he'd want to re-visit.

He reached out to adjust the dial.

'Blazes!' He bellowed. *'Get off it ye mangy feckin' hoor.'* Jumping up, he threw the nearest thing to hand at the cause of his vexation. The flying bowl missed the speeding target by half the width of the kitchen.

Not looking so healthy now was it? No! Just a soggy mess on the floor. 'Ah well,' he thought, 'some you win, most you lose, no one wins 'em all.'

The sudden burst of activity tumbled over the milk jug. The contents sloshed across the table-top making the newspaper unreadable. Some dribbled to the floor, but most of it soaked through the front of his trousers. The guilty moggy disappeared beneath the dresser.

Gritting his teeth, he snarled. 'Bugger! Great! 'Just feckin' great! Welcome back to the real world, Sammy boy.'

Clenching his fists, he counted slowly to ten, it didn't work, he still swore vengeance on the cat. Clean it up or leave it? It wouldn't be fair to the old woman. Not that she'd ever complain. Ten minutes later, with the wreckage cleared, the jumbled thoughts in his head were bobbing like corks in water. *Not a day to be indecisive. Think logically. Clean trousers? Had he any? Yes.*

He took a step backwards and turned towards the door. Squelch! Damn! Soaked through to his underwear. Thank God for his mother. The woman was a treasure. Everything was where it should be. A change of clothes wouldn't be a problem.

Half-way down a freshly brewed mug of sweet tea, he pondered on his situation. It didn't make for good thoughts. Life. Well it hadn't really been much of a lucky straw. Now into the autumn of his sixties, there wasn't a lot of prospects knocking about for aged career criminals. Ex-criminals. The thrill had gone. Somewhere between that mythical rock and a very long drop, he'd decided he no longer had the zest for it. The old ways were gone. No denying it, they'd been good, but things had changed. Stupid bloody kids. Smart-arse little bastards. Now it was all about violence. Guns, knives, drugs and mortuary slabs, in roughly that order. There was nothing at all about living and enjoying life.

Sure, he'd been a villain, but he'd never physically hurt anyone. Violence wasn't in his nature. Banks and insurance jerkoffs might be legal in the eyes of the law, but under the surface they were no better than him. A thief by any other name is still a thief. Living at home was far from idyllic, but after his last government funded vacation, what choice did he have?

His once, so-very-loving missus, hadn't been too long about giving him the elbow. She'd spread her favours around fast enough. The locks had been changed on the marital home, quicker than the cell door had closed behind him, and she'd moved in some sort of poncey hairdresser type. What sort of cunning, conniving, back-stabbing bitch would do that? Right at that minute his options were decidedly limited, but he'd be damned if he'd go down without a fight. Just let 'em see if he would.

The phone in his shirt pocket buzzed. No small talk, just a two-word message, delivered in a hoarse whisper. *'Wishful Dreamer.'* The phone burred, replacing the disembodied voice. The kitchen swam before his eyes and he wobbled as if struck by an attack of vertigo.

Oh Yes! Yes! Yes! Yes! Oh ye good thing! This was it. No doubt about it. This was the day the proverbial chickens came home to roost. The day the turkey (aka) bookie, was about to be plucked. He punched the air with delight. Bad humour dissipated.

The voice of the newsreader interrupted his elation. In pauses between swallowing his tablets and gulping mouthfuls of water, he listened. Just the same old-same-old, most of it passed him by. '...dense fog also caused a multi-vehicle pile- up, blocking the south-bound lane of the M8 at the approach to the toll plaza at Watergrasshill. Police and ambulances at the scene. Long delays expected, avoid if possible. Snow expected later, as the cold snap looks set to continue. Temperatures to plummet further overnight...'

Suddenly the announcer got his undivided attention.

'After an early morning course inspection, racing at Kempton will go ahead as scheduled this afternoon. First of the seven-race card is due to start at 12.40.'

As he turned the corner on to Hollygrove Rd. the clock-tower bells were tinkling melodiously. The sound echoing back and forth between the black slate and red-tiled rooftops. Scudding clouds against a backdrop of lead-grey skies hurried across a sky that was set to go nowhere. He'd always liked walking down here. Not one of the showpiece roads, but it was his kind of place. Friendly hard-working people, getting on with their lives and dealing with whatever vagaries of fate, life threw at them. A good place to put down roots.

A dark-skinned woman was busy cleaning windows. She was humming some Caribbean calypso rhythm as she worked. Her hips swaying to the sounds inside her head. She moved her bucket aside. He passed, wishing he was thirty years younger, and flashed a smile at her. She beamed back, white teeth and good humour. 'Just shakin' my booty Papa.' Suddenly cheered, he laughed. She laughed with him. It was that kind of place.

He threw a side-long glance at one of her freshly polished windows. The image that stared back at him had exactly the look he'd been hoping to project. The double-breasted overcoat, fashionably long, matched the dark-grey trilby to a nicety. His father had just about nailed it right with one of the last bits of wisdom he'd preached at him. At least the words hadn't been wasted. *When you're flat out on the bottom son, make it seem as if you're looking down from the stars.'*

Sammy was hurrying. What his mother would euphemistically describe as *'in a bit of a tear.'*

Thronging the pavements, the pace of the late morning shoppers dictated his speed. Freezing breath rose in the December air as adrenaline pumped through his veins, and for what must have been the twentieth time, he pushed his way between baby buggies and their gossiping owners. *'What the hell was with people.'* He thought. *Christmas shopping! Huh! Had they nothing better to do with their time?*

Huddled from the cold in a shopping-mall doorway, a bundle of beige duffle coats, were masquerading as a school choir. With more enthusiasm than ability a young female teacher went through the motions of conducting her charges. She waved her hands. A dozen or so out-of-tune voices launched cheerfully into the murder of *'Good King Wenceslas.'* Sammy, ignoring the collection box pushed under his nose, sidestepped the acne faced collector and strode on. 'Bloody nuisance.' He thought.

'…and a very Merry Christmas to you too, asshole.' The disgruntled youth muttered at his departing back.

Stop! At the next road-crossing, just as he'd sighted his destination across the street, a guard on point duty gave priority to traffic. Under his breath, Sammy cursed him solidly. It was a wasted effort. The authoritative figure at the centre of the junction obviously knew nothing of or couldn't have cared less about his haste. Raging, he waited. Exhaust fumes hung low to the ground as traffic sped east and bumper-to-bumper, crawled west. Just as suddenly as it started, traffic stopped. The long- arm-of-the-law gave right-of-way to pedestrians. Crowds on the crossing parted before him as if sensing his urgency. With a burst of agility that would have made him a contender for gold anywhere, he flung himself on to the opposite pavement and entered the betting shop.

A quick glance at the wall-clock alleviated his panic. 12.09 Phew! Relief washed over him. That gave him leeway of two full hours of before *Wishful Dreamer* brought home the turkey.

To the right and left of him, like combatants, punters, were readying themselves for battle. All sorts, all ages, from every walk of life. Fresh faced youths, to those with the cement-grey features of troglodytes. They wrestled with racing papers. Notes were jotted down, then compared to information on the flickering screens.

Moving down the room, he found himself a seat and prepared to wait it out.

Kempton! His eyes finally settled on the screen he wanted. Slower than he believed possible the runners, riders and trainers scrolled down the screen. Damn! No starting prices showing as-of-yet. As he tried to mask his mounting excitement he desperately needed to pee.

At last, after a break for a sponsor's advert, the screen scrolled again. Great! *Wishful Dreamer* opened at 33/1, almost a rank outsider. Digging the wad of cash from his pocket took time. Before he could make it to the counter the price had tumbled. 28/1. Still not bad. He lashed the bundle of €50.00 notes on to the counter and muttered his instructions to the clerk. Job done. The price dropped another three points.

He'd scanned the screens with the passion of the possessed. In the seconds before the flag came down, punters on the course threw caution to the winds. Someone lashed £10,000 on the nose. The price plummeted. He'd stared open mouthedly as *Wishful Dreamer* finished at 7/2. A barely beaten second. What in the hell had gone wrong? It was inconceivable it could have happened, but it had. Disgusted, he'd thrown his crumpled betting slip in the bin. The door slammed shut behind him and he vowed never to return.

To an onlooker, it might have looked as if a drunken man had staggered from the door and lurched against the wall. The ice-cold air of the street cut him like a whiplash, but it was the overwhelming sense of failure that was causing the tears to sting his eyelids. An answer eluded him. He banged his forehead against the wall in a frustrated effort to understand. The bloody horse had carried his proverbial shirt on its back, all €850.00 of it. Just to be beaten by a donkey in a photo finish.

He cursed the jockey, trainer and the imbecile that had given the horse that stupid name. Only for having forgotten his travel pass he'd have jumped on a bus to *Wherever* and strangled his informant, slowly. What was it his father had preached? *Always leave a backdoor open, never be without a Plan B.* He'd always had an alternative, effective under normal circumstances, but what had just happened was exceptional. No! Even if having a proper shuffle through the papers was half the battle, it was too damn late to study the *Racing Post.* Tomorrow was another day. He'd just have to suck it up and get on with it.

Retracing his steps, he re-crossed at the junction. The duffle coats and the NYPD choir were locked together in the *Fairy-Tale of New York.* He hated that bloody song. The pimply-faced collector retreated at his approach.

It was 2.30 and Thursday. A visit to the doctor had been put on hold for far too long. He'd intended to give it a miss, but could it make the day any worse? Nothing would make him forget, but maybe a tonic would help him sleep.

Only one voice could be heard from the waiting room, male and loud. Entering, he did a rapid head count, only four, he decided to stay. Seating himself on a vacant chair by the far wall, he waited. A fibre-optic Christmas tree in the corner alternated from red to silver to green and back again.

The voice was loud, too loud. Damn Yuppie! He had all the ingredients, pin-stripe suit, gelled hair and a briefcase. One of those damn phone gadgets was stuck in an ear. The name escaped him for a moment. Bluetooth! That was it. A bloody stupid place to have a tooth, but there was no accounting for some people.

A child of indeterminate sex was clinging to the knees of a heavily pregnant young woman seated opposite him. The woman's make-up might have been applied with a trowel, but it failed to disguise her damaged face. Two eyes, bruised every shade of purple, studied the pattern on the worn linoleum with pretended interest. Why did the *Season to be Jolly* always have to bring some people a shedload of trouble? The child stared at Sammy through eyes as round as saucers.

An elderly lady sat against the window, staring through tortoise-shell spectacles. From a bag at her feet, Holy Mary blue wool, snaked inch-by-inch to a pair of needles clutched in alabaster white fingers.

Picking up a magazine he flicked through to the cross-words. Lovely! Some dipstick had started it, in that they'd filled in all the empty spaces with noughts and crosses.

The Christmas tree pinged and blew a fuse, seconds before the gas heater stuttered, spluttered and went out.

Guffawing loudly, Mr. Bluetooth speed-dialled yet another number. The knitting needles of the old lady clicked away the minutes.

Bang! A hatch on the wall opened and a girl with the voice of *Shirley Temple* announced that the doctor had an emergency call-out. Surgery would re-commence on Friday morning at 9.30. No apology.

Outraged, the yuppie started to protest. Staring blankly at him, *'Shirley Temple'* slammed the hatch shut. Sammy exited on to the street. Darkness was being chased by a north-east wind whistling about the chimney pots as daylight started to fade. He was about to step from the footpath when the engine of a powerful car roared. It u-turned away from the kerbside, spinning wheels and burning rubber. Grinning at Sammy and raising a middle finger in a derisory salute, Mr. Bluetooth, ignoring the honking horns and screeching brakes of the narrowly missed, sped away towards the town centre.

Blazes! What the hell was that about? Shaken, but un-hurt, he staggered back against the wall. Bugger it all to hell. A large coffee was needed. Black with plenty sugar, that might just restore his equilibrium. At least he'd held back enough to pay for that.

Steam rose to the ceiling from the scalding coffee. He warmed his fingers on the mug and sitting back he began taking stock of his situation. The hole he'd dug was deep, but a lifetime of experience told him not to panic. Problem? No money. Solution? Get some. Sooner rather than later. Preferably rather a lot of it. He glanced to where his watch should be. Gone. Sold for a fraction of its value to finance that mornings disastrous escapade. Think! Every problem has a solution.

The waitress, pretty, blonde and Lithuanian with legs that seemed to go on forever, was smiling at him. He smiled back wistfully and supposed she was working for tips.

Should he try the dogs? No! Like women, he'd never had any luck with them. Fuck. Why hadn't he thought of it?

As if in receipt of an epiphany, the answer struck him like a thunderbolt. Prayer was the answer. That was all was left. His mother was always going on about it. Not that it ever did her any good, but it never did any harm either. He racked his brains. Who were the two pillocks she favoured the most? He had 'em. St. Anthony was good; St. Jude might be better. Did it matter? They were big guns. If he fired a shot across their bows, he'd get a response. If he didn't his mother would hear about it. Whew! Why had it taken him so long? Saints. That was the answer. He loved them.

The tension drained from him. Swallowing the last dregs of coffee, he tipped the still smiling *'Miss Lithuania'* his last fiver and headed for the door.

Pre-Christmas browsers, shoppers and some early evening revellers passed on either side. All ignored him. Illuminated by fairy lights, he stood watching a display of flat-screen televisions. Screens of every size beamed out the early evening news. Was it only this morning he'd been hoping to buy his mother one? Now! No hope.

Across the bottom of two dozen screens the text ribbon flickered. For a moment he couldn't, refused to believe, what he was watching. He'd difficulty focussing as he tried to peer through his vaporising breath. There was no audio feed, but that made no difference, he could read the words. '...after an incident at Kempton Park races this afternoon, in a totally unexpected decision, a stewards enquiry was reversed. The race has been awarded to the 7/2 shot *Wishful Dreamer* winner of the 2.20. All other results st...'

Sammy had seen enough. Jesus! Them saints didn't hang about. In a flurry of wind blowing coat tails he hurried once more across the roadway to the bookies.

'No! No! No! Read my lips. You're not coming in. We're closing.'

Tottering on six-inch stilettos, a lean-as-a-whippet blonde was pushing against the door. Sammy didn't argue, he just pushed harder. The girl stumbled and screamed. From the back office someone cursed and shouted.

Blondie screeched a reply. 'I couldn't stop him sir. He broke in.'

The door of the office was thrown open. Red-faced and indignant, 'Mr. Bluetooth' stood on the threshold. 'What's your problem? Are you deaf? We're closed.'

Sammy took his time, savouring the sweetness... 'so you see my winning docket is somewhere near the bottom of your bin. Now if either of—'

A sneering Blondie interrupted. 'Dream on old man. We don't do garbage searches.'

Picking up the bin, Sammy dumped the contents on the floor. 'You do now.'

This was something 'Mr. Bluetooth' couldn't comprehend. Ashen faced, he mouthed to the blonde. 'Do it. Do it now.'

Glaring at Sammy, she waved a talon-like finger in his face. Fit to spit venom, she shrieked. *'IF I BREAK A NAIL, YOU PAY. UNDERSTOOD?'*

Three and a half minutes, later 'Mr. Bluetooth' took on the mannerisms of a beached fish. He stabbed the buttons on a calculator. *'Oh fuck! Oh Jesus! Th-tha-th-that's...'*

'A lot of money' Sammy finished. '€24,650. To be exact.'

A slack-jawed Blondie stared goggle-eyed at the docket clutched between the trembling fingers of her speechless boss. What it was she didn't quite know, but somehow the old boy seemed to have put one over on that pompous asshole she called sir.

Ten minutes later with €24.000 secreted in his coat, Sammy prepared to leave. About to trouser the remaining cash, he paused, peeling off a €50 note, he held it out. 'Here ye are Sweetheart, on the way home do yourself a favour, buy the rest of that skirt. Merry Christmas.'

'Par rap a rum pum pum a rum…' The choir was mangling *The Little Drummer Boy*. A smiling Sammy stuck another €50 into the tin of the pimply-faced collector. Through a break in the clouds a shooting star vanished behind the roof tops. He felt a spring in his step that he hadn't felt for ages. Could life get any better? For him, the *Miracle of Christmas* had come true. Somewhere up there, shielded by darkness, there was a God.

A distant light cast eerie shadows over the street. Lying by the roadside, the crumpled body held the attention of the dark-clad figures standing on the kerb.

A traffic tail-back caused by rubberneckers, was being directed past the scene. On duty, a guard wearing a high-viz vest and wielding a torch, appeared to have everything as it should be, well in hand. The siren of a speeding ambulance wailed a warning of its approach.

'What happened?'

The question came from a tall man wearing the insignia of a sergeant on the shoulders of his tunic. 'I'm not really sure Sergeant, but it seems likely that it was an accident. The driver says she couldn't avoid him. Says he came out of nowhere. She's badly shocked and in the circumstances it's understandable. If you want a word, she's sitting in the patrol car. I said we'd take a statement later.'

'Breathalysed?'

'Yes. Negative.'

'Good man. You did well. Any ID on the victim?'

'No Sergeant, but I'm not long stationed here, only drafted in for Christmas really, I wouldn't know anyone hereabouts, but perhaps you might.'

'Yes! No car. He'll be local. I'll take a look. One thing Sergeant. He was carrying quite a bundle of cash. Thousands I'd say. He must have struck it lucky somewhere. Nothing else in his pockets, just two receipts. One from that big electronic place on the precinct. Appears he paid cash for a top-of-the-range flat-screen telly, only an hour ago. There's an address. It's supposed to be delivered and fitted tomorrow, Christmas Eve. The other is for a luxury hamper of Christmas goodies to go to the Welfare Home on Viaduct Street.'

The Sergeant wasn't listening. 'Well, well, well. If it isn't Sammy Barr.' He muttered. 'You know him Sergeant?'

There was a sadness in the Sergeant's voice as he answered.

'Yes son. I know him. Have done for years. Sammy here was legend when I was fresh out of the training depot. He's been straight now for a while, but he pulled the wool over our eyes often enough. We knew he planned and carried out some bloody huge jobs, but there was never a shred of proof, like Teflon, nothing stuck to the bugger.'

'You sound like you respect him Sergeant?'

'Yes, I do boy. In time you'll learn that men like Sammy

– 31 –

Barr don't cross your path every day. He was as old school as they come. When violence and drugs became the order of the day, he wanted no part of that life anymore. If you learn nothing else this Christmas, learn respect, because a man like this deserves it.'

Stooping, the Sergeant picked up the battered trilby and placed it on the body. Gusting winds brought the first flurries of snow. In moments the powdery flakes shrouded his remains. A bulb popped as a camera flashed. The scene was captured for the morning papers.

'Poor old fellow.' Someone muttered. 'If he was a betting man, he'd have enjoyed coming out in a photo-finish.'

The Man from the Council

'Can you spare a few minutes?'

The man from the council called on Friday. I had just put my dogs in the car and was about to depart for the day. 'Can you spare a few minutes my good man?' Says he.

'Indeed I can,' Says I. 'I can spare all day if you like.'

'No,' says he. 'A few minutes will do the finest.'

'Right!' Says I. 'What's the problem?'

The man from the Council looked over my shoulder at the distant range of the Nagle mountains. 'The news is not the best.' Says he. 'In fact, truth be told, it's bad.'

'Hello! Has somebody died?' Says I. 'How bad is bad?'

'The worst kind.' Says he. 'We were doing the sums back in the office, making calculations and such like, and I'll tell you now we reckon you've four leaks in the vicinity of your water meter.'

'That's bad.' Says I.

'It is.' Says he. 'Lord God man! It's very bad. The only way it could get any worse is if them Bosnians bate us on Monday night. Now that would be a disaster.'

As this nugget of logic fell, I had to draw a few deep breaths and do some serious thinking. Then I said nothing. The man from the council continued.

'Four leaks. Two and two.' Says he, pointing in the general direction of anywhere.

'I'll take it two and two doesn't amount to four,' Says I.

'You're on the ball,' says he. 'There's eighteen thousand

gallons of water a day shooting like blazes through your meter every twenty-four hours, twenty-four seven. That's a powerful waste of water.'

'What's that in litres?' Says I.

'Ninety thousand, give or take a litre or two, and it's flowing beneath our feet as we speak. That's a million litres every twelve days and you'll have to agree that it couldn't get much worse than that.'

'Where's it all going to?' Says I.

'Damned if I know,' says he, 'but it's not coming out of your taps so nothing for you to worry about. Anyway we've a crew coming on this morning to fix them.'

'Hold on,' says I. 'Those four leaks were fixed about three years back by the council.'

'Indeed they were,' says he, 'but truth be told, the fellow that did the job back then was a plumber in name only. Useless would be too kind a word for him. This time things will be different.'

I waited for an hour. The promised crew never arrived. The water-meter man checked his watch. 'I think they must have stopped off for the tea before starting.' Says he.

When later that evening I returned, I found the leaks had indeed been fixed. Fast forward to Monday morning, the man from the council was back.

'Can you move the car my good man?' Says he.

'I can,' says I, 'Is there a problem?'

'You might say that.' Says he. 'The road is going to have to come up.'

I moved the car. Moved it in the nick of time, as John Charles Bamford's famous invention the J.C.B. led the charge to my garden wall. This was followed by a truck and two vans.

True to form the flasks sandwiches and a copy of the Sun were produced, and the real work of the day commenced. To give credit where it's due, once those boys swung into action, there was no stopping. The tarmac was cut, a trench dug, a new pipe laid and the whole lot back-filled in no time. Even resurfaced with new asphalt and a good job done too.

How's that for you?

Tuesday. The man from the council was back. This time a different man. He read the meter and gave me the figures.

'Keep a record of them,' says he, 'with the time and date.'

'I will,' says I, 'at least Bosnia didn't bate us.'

He gave me a strange sort of look. 'What's that got to do with anything?' Says he.

Oops! Wrong man. The man from the council departed. Me! I crawled back beneath my duvet to wrestle with dreams of leaking meters and battles with Irish Water or whatever alias they'll be operating under by that time. Ah well! '*Sin sceal eile,*' as they say, it's a story for another day.

'Tweedle' Dee Comes of Age
'Now it's someone else's turn'

'Well that must rank as one of the stupidest schemes you've ever come up with. It's certainly hit a new low, even for you. I thought you'd have grown out of all that stuff. How wrong could I be? You should know all that war business is just for kids, and it's anything but a game. Is there nothing at all of use connecting your feckin' ears?'

The old man snorted. It was sound that might have been mistaken for a laugh. It wasn't.

Christy 'Tweedle' Dee had looked at the speaker, startled at the anger in his voice, but the old man hadn't finished. He paused just long enough to swallow a mouthful of something from a hip flask. Then he grimaced and spat into the sawdust between his feet before glaring through his one good eye.

'Hah! Is it any wonder I've a lip on me for liquor? Jaysus Christy! You've come up with some cock-eyed schemes, but this takes the bloody biscuit. Have you not got a modicum of common sense at all? What about your ma? Have you discussed this with her?'

Eyes averted to the floor; Christy shook his head from side to side.

'No? How did I guess? Don't you think she should have more than a passing interest in your future, or lack of it? Show her some respect lad. She's an intelligent woman.'

This time Christy nodded.

'Hmmm! I'll take it that's a yes. So tell me, what's it to be? Let me carry the can for you as always, is it? Well this time *'Danny Boy'* says no. Don't you go forgetting it.'

It had been a long time ago, but Christy hadn't forgotten. Recollection came easy, as the years rolled back. He leaned on the spade, not really sure what he was wiping from his eyes. Was it the soft rain, sweat or tears?

With the benefit of hindsight it was easy to see how right the old man had been, but then, hadn't he been working on the wisdom of experience. His idea had been simple, but as usual he'd never taken the opposition to his best laid plans into account.

It was in the village shop that he'd first heard about the war in Spain. When the gossips realised he was present, the voices would drop to a whisper.

'Best say nothing in front of him,' they'd say. *'The lad can't help it, but he's not right in the head.'*

Every time he'd heard snippets of news, he'd been held enthralled. The war had started in mid-July. Rumour had it that young men of his age were being recruited. It was no secret that a stranger had arrived on the once-a-week train from the city. Hadn't the pony and trap belonging to the banker collected him from the station? Fuelled by the coachman, rumours had run faster than a dose of salts through the village. The outcome of the nudges, winks and wild speculation, resulted in the stranger being proclaimed to be a recruiting officer for General O'Duffy. Which, strange as it may have seemed, was indeed true.

Christy had watched. Concealed amidst the foliage of an overhanging tree, he'd looked on as the stranger, wearing a new blue shirt and armband had drilled the chosen ones in a field near the village. In place of rifles, hurling sticks were the weapons of choice being aimed at imaginary enemies. At a shouted order, a ragged chorus of 'bangs' echoed around the field. Christy thought the young man with the stutter, who helped the blacksmith in the forge above at the crossroads, done a very fine impression of a machine gun.

Christy knew about Spain. He knew someone that lived there. Well, he didn't exactly know him. Not with the same easy familiarity that he knew his mother and 'Danny Boy', but it was much the same. He was in a book. He had to be important. *Don Quixote* lived there. One of the few people he'd found of interest during the six-years drudgery he'd endured through primary school. A larger than life hero, who lived life on a knife edge. He fought battles with the strangest kind of enemies and championed the causes of the underdog. Could anything be better than to travel to Spain and fight alongside him? Nothing! If there was Christy didn't know of it.

He'd volunteered. Not that he'd ever say that to 'Danny Boy.' He didn't have to. That man seemed to have the inside track on everything. In too short a time the entire village seemed to know his business.

He'd approached the son of the banker, a self-important skinful of pomposity, who seemed to view those he considered beneath him through a permanent sneer. That same sneer was directed at Christy when he made his request. He'd just laughed at him for his impertinence and made him the joke of the week around the neighbourhood. Christy hadn't minded. When he'd realised he'd have joined the wrong side, being the butt of a joke was a small price to pay for rejection. No way would *Don Quixote* have fought on the side of… What the hell had *'Danny Boy'* called them? *Fascist bastards.* Yes! That was it.

He spat on his hands and dug another spadeful of the thick yellow clay from the unyielding ground. Yes! *Fascist bastards.* That had a ring to it. He didn't doubt *'Danny Boy'* knew about war. He'd been just a lad of sixteen when he'd gone to fight in the great war.

'I was a damn fool,' he'd said. Hell bent on making the same mistake you want to make now. Think I'm going to stand by and let that happen? Think again. I was one of the lucky ones; in that I only lost an eye. To this day I don't know why.'

He'd spat. The reddish-brown tobacco juice stained the sawdust and shavings at his feet. 'Someday you'll be a man,' he'd said. 'I only hope you stay alive long enough to enjoy it.'

Christy had listened. Getting more demoralized by the minute as the story unfolded. He struggled to comprehend how dehumanised people could become when caught up in the reality of war.

'Great War! What damn fool came up with that load of horse-shite? No one that had been on the Somme, and that's for sure. No doubt he got himself a medal anyway. Did he wallow knee deep in the filth of the trenches, choking on the stench of gangrene from the dead and dying, or lie for days on end soaking in his own piss? All the while being eaten alive by flies and lice. Did he see his mates hanging like scarecrows from the barbwire that criss-crossed *No-Mans-Land* until the flesh rotted off their bones? I don't think so. If he did *Great* is not a word he would have used. That's the thinking of them in high places, and believe me, those people don't think like us. They think that treating the minions like participants in a dog and pony show and throwing a few medals about will make everything alright. Does it hell!

Answer me this. What's so bloody great about the wholesale slaughter of men and boys? Little more than children most of us were, and we died there by the thousand. Makes you laugh, does it? I hope not! Because it ought to make you bloody cry.'

Christy hadn't been laughing. He thought he might never laugh again. What he'd heard wasn't the way things were supposed to be. This was brutal. Amidst the carnage, there was precious little heroism and where was the glory?

'*Danny Boy*' continued. 'If you were to lean on that damn spade 'til Doomsday you couldn't count all those killed, and maybe those that died were the lucky ones. It was all about dying, but in some ways surviving was worse. For the five months on the Somme, blood mixed with mud, as we killed them, and they killed us. When they'd finished plucking lumps of steel out of my hide and shrapnel had taken my eye, I was sent home. Someone was praying for me, because to this day I count myself lucky to have survived. Now twenty years later I still have the stench of death in my nostrils, and I wake at night to the screams of the dying and maimed. Believe me boy, there has to be a better way.

One day them bastards that started it shook hands and sent us home. It was all for nothing. Did the likes of you or me get a better life because of it? Did it make the world a better place? Don't answer that.'

Almost affectionately he'd placed a bony hand on Christy's shoulder, squeezing it gently. 'No! Don't go. You've got no idea what it will be like over there. It's father against son in Spain. Brother fighting brother. It happened here one time and it's the worst type of war. The unity and love of families divided forever. Believe me, that's something you don't want to live with. Civil! Whatever bloody idiot called it that got it wrong as well. There's damn all that's civil about war. What use is a medal? You can't eat it. To get awarded one only goes to show what an idiot you were to have gone there in the first place. When you haven't got a hand to wipe your backside and your legs have been shot away, come back then and tell me it was worth it. If you ever come back at all.'

Christy had stared at the worn toes of his boots. There had to be a hole somewhere he could crawl into and die.

The old man continued. 'If I'd my life back again d'ye think I'd go? If I'd known back in the day what I know now I'd be running so fast you wouldn't see my heels for dust.'

Christy hadn't gone. He'd heard that seven hundred and fifty men recruited by O'Duffy had gone to fight alongside the government forces. Two hundred and fifty more had rallied to the call of Frank Ryan to stand against them and defend the rights of the Spanish workers. Odds of only 3/1. *Don Quixote* would have laughed.

Christy continued to hack at the clay. He piled it in a mound beside himself and cursed as some of it clung like lead weights to his boots. The ground was hard, but the hole had to be deep. After a struggle, a rock, like a broken tooth, yielded to the pressure of the spade and broke free of the ground. Cursing again, he tossed it to one-side. St. Brigids Cross was old; a village typical of its time. Nobody knew just how old, or why it ever been given that name seeing as it wasn't even on a crossroads. It was the sort of place where mongrel dogs gave warning of strangers; cats snoozed on window ledges and chickens perched on top of open half-doors. It was little more than a higgeldy-piggledy collection of houses that had somehow grown haphazardly along both sides of a riverbank. A few (very few) were distinct from their neighbours, in that they were regularly painted and were adorned with slate roofs. These were the dwellings of the banker and the doctor, who commuted daily to the nearest sizeable town.

The great majority of houses were still clad in the traditional straw thatch. Thatch, that was in most cases falling into decay and covered with a thick layer of ancient green moss. It did have a church, as had mostly every Irish village. A grey-stone building which stood on the only piece of high ground in the area. Next to it was a two-teacher primary school, built from the same grey rock. It also had a general store that doubled as a post office and as well as stamps, sold everything from groceries to hardware. A small stone bridge connected both sides of the river. The road to the nearest town meandered along one bank, while the village on the other side was little more than a green area surrounded with dwellings that gave the initial impression that they were leaning drunkenly one on the other. There was very little colour. Just grey stone walls, faded thatch, and the green of moss and ivy that clung to every surface.

Just outside the village was the single-track, one platform railway station. Once a day a tired sounding train puffed in, clanging noisily against the buffers with the hissing of steam and the squealing of brakes. An hour later it departed, to the waving of a green flag and the lonesome sound of the guard's whistle.

A few hundred yards on the southern edge of the village, or the shot of a well-thrown bowl beyond the station stood a very neatly kept white-washed cottage. This was where Christy Dee lived with his mother. The end of the rainbow never hovered near to the house. A few times it had come close, but there was never a crock of gold; at least if there was, he'd never found it.

'Danny Boy' was … ? Well, *'Danny Boy'.* He lived in his own place on just the other side of the boundary wall. The best anyone could say about him was that on the finest day of summer he was just as cantankerous as he'd be on the wettest day of winter. It had been heard said that he'd rather spit than salute. He never suffered fools gladly, he just never suffered them at all. When he'd a pound going spare, he was well known to have a penchant for strong liquor.

A carpenter by trade, and no doubt a craftsman of the highest calibre, he eked out a living of sorts in a workshop at the back of his house. Unfortunately, he was possessed of a trait, in that he was decidedly choosey about who he worked for. Before accepting a commission, he'd have to satisfy himself as to the merits of a prospective customer. If rejected, a client knew not to return, so his customer base was decidedly small.

He'd always had a liking for Christy. There were some that wondered why? Others claimed to know. The truth was nobody knew for certain, but the ploughshare wasn't forged that could scratch the bond between them.

There was those that considered him misfortunate in be-ing born, as they said, *on the wrong side of the blanket.* It never bothered him. True! There were times when he'd wondered what it would be like to have a father. These were far outweighed by the times he'd thought he'd been very lucky.

Not a lot of difference really, just that men lived with the mothers of other children, his mother didn't live with a man. A big advantage in that, because no one had to hide in terror when the blindness of an alcohol fuelled rage took precedence over a morsel of common sense. A voice was never heard to be raised in anger behind the door of Emily Dee's cottage.

Other children got stuff at Christmas and birthdays; he didn't, but that never made him feel in any way deprived. Did other boys have a fox that was tame enough to sleep in a basket at the foot of the bed? Did any of them have a whole variety of birds come when he whistled to pick some seeds and breadcrumbs from his palm?

For six long years Christy drifted through an education system where indifference was the order of the day. Teachers had important work to do; how could they be expected to waste something as precious as time on a fatherless ragamuffin?

What use would he ever make of an education? Didn't the son of the banker or the doctor's daughter deserve the best they could provide? Sometime in the future they'd be people of importance in the community. Maybe they'd aspire to the heady goal of politics and become leaders of the nation? They were the children that surely merited the benefits of schooling; not the toe-rag from the cottages. Someone of that ilk was best ignored. He'd felt hurt; what child wouldn't? Outsiders never saw his tears.

He'd been confirmed into the faith during his 6th year in the system after reading with great difficulty the green paperback Catechism from cover-to-cover. Love and understanding confused him. What was all that about? Love thy neighbour! Who did that? Nobody he knew, he was certain of that.

Naïvely he'd gone through with the charade, in the mistaken belief that as a *Soldier of Christ* his lot might improve; it hadn't. At the very least he thought he might get to wear a uniform; he didn't.

To the relief of the school board it was his last day of formal education. Christy Dee was spewed out of the system.

The seasons withered much like fallen leaves, as the years drifted past the door. There were births, marriages and deaths; events that affected the lives of people.

The banker's son had married the daughter of the doctor. He'd come back from Spain with a medal on his chest, no legs, and a drink problem. Christy had often listened to him whining as his wife pushed him in a wheelchair along the river road. A blanket always covered where his lower limbs had been. Three years hadn't passed since the war had started, and the still childless doctor's daughter had aged two decades.

He thought back to the day he'd gone to the station to watch the newly trained recruits depart. Seventeen would-be heroes had marched down the platform, proud and straight. At the head of the throng of watching onlookers the banker and his wife had led the cheers as they'd watched the doctor's daughter embrace their son and kiss him a fond goodbye. A minute later he'd waved triumphantly from the carriage doorway as the guard waved the green flag and blew his whistle. In the instant that his eyes met Christy's, it might have been a trick of the light, but the smile seemed to change to a sneer. Enveloped in a cloud of steam the train departed.

During the Spring of '39 five had returned; all bore the scars of the conflict. He'd watched with *Danny Boy'* as they'd been helped from the train; crippled, blind and maimed.

The old man hadn't said much. 'Half a million people have died since that war started. Three years later and it's changed damn all. What day did they decide to call an end to it? April 1st boy. Fool's Day, that in itself should tell you something.'

A brass band had been brought from the town for the occasion, but after the first few notes, the music died away. The doctor's daughter passed. Looking neither right nor left, eyes fixed firmly on the cobbles of the platform. Too worn to weep, she'd pushed her husband towards the station gates. The banker and his wife followed; heads bowed. There was no cheering. The late Spring sunshine highlighted the tears on their cheeks. Christy imagined he could feel their sorrow. '

Danny Boy' had shaken his head from side-to-side as the old couple passed. 'War changes nothing boy. It won't be too long before some other fools swap places with those two and send another young man off to waste his life, and for what? It's not right to speak badly of anyone, but they've done their bit for stupidity now it'll be the turn of someone else. It never feckin' ends.

Danny Boy' had been right. A short while later Hitler's troops had invaded Poland and the world had plunged into hell.

The ground was dug; he threw down his spade and stretched his muscles. The old man had died at the weekend. He'd been shaping a spoke for a cartwheel, then he was on the ground, cradled by wood shavings and sawdust. Dead.

They'd cried then, just the two of them. Mother and son, grieving for a man that in some peculiar way had brought unity to their lives.

In the workshop Christy had done exactly as he'd seen the old man do for more years than he could remember. He'd selected the coffin boards, choosing carefully the very best for the job. It took a few days, but when finished he felt he'd done a job that the old man would be proud of. A final sanding, before he carved the panel that bore the name, *'Danny Boy.'*

Then he'd gone to see the priest.

'No! He didn't own a grave. Had he money? Yes! How much?'

Not a lot, but enough, just about enough. The translucent fingers of the priest closed on the crumpled banknotes. He was shown a plot by a ditch at a point furthest from the church. He'd open the grave himself.

'Fair enough. Friday morning 11 o'clock; don't be late.' The priest shook some Holy Water on the weed-covered ground and walked away.

He'd dug the grave as he thought it should be, deep, as the old man would deserve. Nobody came. There was just himself and his mother, the priest and a few men he'd brought from the village. Strangers. He'd have preferred if they hadn't come.

Half-way through the prayers some rain spattered off the coffin, then a loud peal of thunder smothered the sounds of the chapel bell and the rain fell in torrents. It ran from his mother's headscarf and seemed to fill her eyes with tears.

Before running for shelter, the priest rushed through a decade of the rosary and muttered something in Latin. Christy could have buried the old man himself; he weighed no more than a bird.

Three weeks later, on a sleepy afternoon, at the local post office, a well-dressed stranger presented himself. The enquiry was simple; where would he find Christy.

'You now know the story. It appears that your friend, on his passing, left you in quite comfortable circumstances. He sold off his property some time ago and left you the proceeds. It amounts to a rather sizeable sum of money. The workshop and tools are also yours.'

He held out a card he'd extracted from his wallet. 'We would, of course, be happy to represent you at any time.'

A long week had passed before his mother handed him a tattered brown envelope. The original address had been scratched out. Now in the old familiar scribble it bore the single word, *'Christy.'*

The photograph inside was old, black and white, cracked and frayed around the edges. *'Danny Boy'* he knew at once. His mother had been young then, perhaps mid-twenties, nothing more. She'd been cradling a baby to her breast. He looked at her, studying the tears in her eyes before looking back at the photo.

'A very strange man, your father; he spent his whole time fighting against whatever life choose to throw at him. That same life was never too kind to us, but he did care. He loved you boy; more than anything, he loved you. He made me promise you were never to know until after he was gone. It was just the way of him. Seeing as your twenty-one today, it seemed like the right time to be setting the record straight.'

Christy placed the photo on the mantlepiece. His mother gently squeezed his shoulder as he sat himself before the fire.

'You'll not forget him boy, will you?'

The passing of the old man had, without doubt, created a void, but he wouldn't be forgotten. Christy knew that every time he walked into the workshop, picked up a hammer, shaped a piece of wood or swept up shavings, he'd remember. They'd been forged from gold, all those years they'd been together; why would he want to forget?

He blew, then blew harder. The candles on the small square chocolate cake flickered and went out. *'Tweedle'* Dee became of age.

...As My Mam Says...

Did ye know Maureen O'Hara served me breakfast?

A cheerless sort of a morning, I was thinking to myself. It was, in my opinion, everything a morning shouldn't be. Grey as a badger's bum, accompanied by a drizzle that given time, would work its way through the hide of a horse. That was supposed to be the best bit. Earlier the weather forecaster, with a toothpaste-white smile, had promised there was worse on the way. Lovely. I loved that woman. She was guaranteed to kit me out with a fit of depression every time she appeared.

I was, as is my usual Sunday morning custom, heading down the road for a rendezvous with the breakfast. Good food at a reasonable price. It can't be beaten, especially, if like me, the budget is stretched tighter than the skin on a mountain goat.

In I go. Behind the counter was a very pretty lady with the most magnificent mane of red-hair imaginable. Under the lights it went through the colours of the spectrum. Everything from the russet-red of autumn leaves, to the burnished sheen of well-polished copper. It was breath-takingly stunning. Lucky lady, I was thinking. She smiled a greeting. The clouds rolled back. 'Good morning sir.' Says she. 'What will you have?'

The lady called me sir, (doesn't happen often) the day was looking better already.

'Well first,' says I, 'Tell me, you wouldn't by any chance be a grand-daughter of yer woman in *The Quiet Man*. Her that was the bane of John Wayne's life.'

'Ahh no.' Says she, laughing. 'That's Maureen O'Hara, you'd be talking about. Sure, she was famous. I'm not, though people have said I look like her, as if I'd be so lucky. It must be the hair I suppose.'

'That doesn't surprise me,' says I. 'Sure if you'd been around then, you'd have got the part.'

She beamed. It brightened the moment, the room and the greyness peeping through the window.

'Anyway,' says I. 'Give me the full works, and could I have some extra bacon for the two waiting in the car?'

'Won't they come in?' says she. 'There's nice tables by the windows, not that there's much to see today.'

'In a heartbeat,' says I. 'Only dogs are not allowed.'

'Dogs?' Says she. 'Oh, I'm so sorry now, but that might cause a bit of problem alright.'

To give the lady credit, she served a meal like no other. My shotgun riders, best friend and constant companions, Twister and Buddy, certainly enjoyed chewing the fat that morning.

Five minutes later I'm there, carving a chunk from the best breakfast this side of Heaven, when I heard it. The voice.

With a forkful of sausage on route to its final resting place, I stopped. I listened. Hmmm! It came again. From somewhere below the level of the tabletop. Curiosity got the better of me, I chanced a look.

Mystery solved. 'Hello.' Said the voice.

I found myself staring into the wide-blue eyes of what could only have been a cherub. This little lady might well have been painted by Michelangelo, or she could well have been a Fairy Princess.

'Hello.' She says again. 'I haven't seen you before.'

'Hello yourself young lady.' Says I. 'I don't believe I've seen you before either.'

Rapid fire, with the speed of bullets, questions came thick and fast. 'What's your name? Where do you live? Where's your wife? Why is she not with you?'

She put me through the wringer. I confessed to all. Once back in the Eighties I was held by the Special Branch in Pembroke Dock, South Wales, for routine questioning. I hadn't done anything. Relax. The officer in charge that day could have taken lessons from this girl. She knew it all.

As she'd already elicited my name, she told me hers. I learned that she lived *'up the road'* and that her really bestest friend in the whole world, lived up the road as well. This information was accompanied by a series of gestures. She danced from foot to foot. Heel, toe and back-step. Pirouetted a few times and waved her arms about all over, but the constant stream of chatter never flagged for an instant. It was innocence being joyfully expressed. It was magic in its purest form.

'As my mam says, Sundays a duvet day. She's still asleep. Too tired to get up. Too lazy to come for breakfast. My dad says too much gin last night.'

On tiptoes, she hung off the edge of the table and eye-balled the contents of my plate. I got, what I took to be a withering look, as she dissected what was on offer.

I discovered that my idea of breakfast, was to her eyes, a no-go area, a plate to be avoided, a health hazard. She had thoughts on my chosen path. A bad road I was on, and she was no way shy of telling me. My culinary choices were given the red card.

'Why aren't you having cereal? It would be better for you. Five slices of toast? OMG. That's an awful lot of bread. Is it any wonder you're so fat?' Sausages! She checked, Counting on her fingers. Four. 'Have you any hiding under them beans and all that other stuff.'

'No.' says I. 'There's only the four.'

'Good. As my mam says, them things are bad for you. Do you know they puts all sorts of yucky stuff into them?'

'Now that I know I'll keep it in mind.' Says I.

It went on. ... as my mam says... and then went on some more. The little Princess had an opinion on everything. She was never caught for a word. Eventually she spotted someone else that need the benefit of her wisdom. She wandered away. I laughed until the coffee pot ran dry.

I departed. The interrogation specialist was in the carpark with her dad. She asked could she hug my dogs. Twister, yes. Buddy, no.

'Why not?' I explained. 'He's nervous of children.' Poor old Twister was taken in a headlock that all but strangled him. She showered him with kisses. Squeezed him with hugs. Eventually, he surfaced for some well-deserved gulps of air. The lassie wasn't finished yet. Her parting shot was a gem, and almost brought tears to my eyes.

'Why do you wear a hat?' She answered her own question with another. 'Is it because you've no hair? As my mam says...' Her father intervened. I suspected it was just in the nick of time. 'Shut-up!' You've bothered the man enough.'

I departed, laughing, never having found out what her mam's thoughts were on hairless men. She shouted back. 'Thank you for calling.'

Three years old? I could hardly believe it. Somewhere down the line there's a bright future ahead. ...as her mam would probably say...

That little lady will spread sunshine wherever she goes.

I was laughing all day, even though I never did find out *Maureen O'Hara's'* real name.

The Man in the Black Suit

*He'd come back many times, making demands;
unholy demands*

The large bluebottle passed within a hair's breadth of the young girls neck. God! She hated those things, wasps and bluebottles she could well live without. The constant buzzing irritated her and disturbed her train of thought. Each time it got too close she stopped what she was doing to flick it away. 'Still, summers almost over and they'll be gone soon,' she thought to herself. as she sat with head bowed intent upon her task. The late evening sun shone full strength through the glassless aperture in the wall that served as a window, illuminating the shadowy interior of the cow byre. The single narrow sunbeam played on the head and shoulders of the girl, and she thought that was what had attracted the bluebottle.

She sat precariously on an old three-legged wooden stool; her forehead pressed against the flanks of the docile old cow she was milking. Today her mind was miles away, not at all on the task in hand. The warm body of the cow comforted her and to anyone observing she was a girl that appeared to be happy at her work. Her two hands on the udder of the cow were just a blur and all movements seemed automatic, but her mind was a million miles away. The shiny steel pail gripped between her knees was almost full. Each pull on the cow's teat sent a jet of warm, creamy white milk sluicing through the foam-topped contents of the bucket. She sat there for a long minute, enjoying the feel of the warm sun where it reached her bare neck below the dark green ribbon that tied-up her red-gold hair.

Gazing out the door of the stall, across the yard an old sheepdog was laying full length, stretched in the shade afforded by the spreading branches of a chestnut tree. The sunlight danced on the tree, dappling the leaves with a myriad of shades, all of them green. Like a picture postcard of idyllic rural charm, it was a tranquil, pastoral scene.

The old dog was doing its best to ignore the juvenile antics of young pup intent on interrupting its daydreams. On a normal day the girl would have found such a simple innocent activity amusing, but today she didn't even see it. The pup pulled the old dog's tail and the resulting yelp roused the girl from the tumultuous assortment of thoughts spinning about in her mind.

Placing a hand on the rump of the cow to steady herself, she stood. Across the yard the old dog growled a warning at the frolicsome pup. Placing both hands on her hips the girl stretched and yawned. It had been a long day and it wasn't over yet. She struggled to lift the pail of milk clear of the floor, but the weight of the full bucket was getting too much for her. She'd noticed that these last few weeks and soon she realised she wouldn't manage it at all. These days it was taking all her strength and ingenuity to get it from the floor to the rim of the churn. Everything even simplest of tasks were now a big effort.

She emptied the pail watching as the milk splashed into the ten-gallon churn. There were five of them, all full now, standing in a line waiting for the following morning to be taken to the creamery.

She wiped her hands on the hem of the old printed blue

pinafore that had been passed on to her from the old woman. She wondered what it was like to get something new, all the clothes she had were passed down to her from someone else. Even what she had for best wear, the blouse and skirt, her good Sunday coat and her flat-heeled black walking shoes had once all been worn by strangers.

She loved those shoes. They'd been almost new when the old woman had bargained with the tinker for them a few days before last Christmas. She'd called the tinker a lot of hard names, but after a lot of haggling a bargain was struck. They'd spat in their palms and shook hands. The shoes were hers and the tinker went off with a fat hen and four brown eggs. Each of them lamenting how the other had robbed them, but that was expected and was the way of things.

She still rubbed them down once a week with a greasy bacon bone as this gave them a nice glossy shine and helped to keep them waterproof. From the village church the bell tolled the evening Angelus. She pulled shut the dairy door.

The pup ran at her heels tugging at the hem of the old pinafore. Swallows flashed across the sky, darting and diving about her head as she walked. A solitary magpie perched on an iron-shod wheel of the donkey cart.

The girl walked with a slight limp. It didn't bother her, as the Kelly's had got it seen to years before and now it was not so noticeable at all.

She heard the old woman call from beyond the half door that supper was ready. She shouted a reply.

This evening she wasn't hungry, but she knew she had to go through the motions, keep up the charade and try and make everything look as normal as possible.

A large wooden rain barrel stood by the back door. She

dipped her hands in the brackish water and shook them dry, then kicked the step to knock any heavy mud from her boots before entering the kitchen. The old man was already seated, spreading the thick yellow home-made butter across his bread. He looked up as she entered.

The old woman stood facing the large Aga cooker. She poured the scalding hot water into the teapot, then lifted off the saucepan of eggs and placed them in the centre of the table. Nobody spoke. The old woman sat at the head of the table. her husband on one side, the girl on the other. The old woman crossed herself and muttered a prayer, the old man cracked open the top of an egg with the back of a spoon. A chipped plaster statue of the Blessed Virgin in faded blue and white looked down from a shelf above the radio. The meal was eaten in a silence that was deafening.

After supper the girl washed up; before climbing the rickety old ladder to the attic room above the kitchen where she slept beneath the slates. Lost in thought she sat herself down on the edge of the bed and stared at the Sacred Heart lamp. From a ceiling beam above her head a spider spun a silver web of near-perfect symmetry.

She wondered how old she was, time had no hold on her, this room and this farm was all she knew. She didn't know the year she came here; just that it was in the early fifties; and now it was nineteen sixty-seven; so she supposed she must surely be in her late twenties.

Before this place she had a life, but it took years to forget. She never knew her real parents. Taken from her mother at birth and placed in an orphanage, she didn't know her real name, not to mind her age.

The early years had been hard. Her lame leg was like a

barrier to friendship, the other children shunned her as if her affliction was contagious. The religious order that ran the home were strict, they were for the most part devoid of love and incapable of showing affection. Her existence in the care of the nuns seemed like an eternity. Other children were taken out of it, if they got a chance of a life somewhere with the well-dressed men and women that came on Sunday afternoons.

Not her, the crippled girl was always passed over. After a while, the nuns hadn't put her on display anymore. They'd just lock her in the dormitory when Sunday came around. Not that she minded. It was better than being stared at, and whispered about. The condemning mouths hidden behind the lady's linen handkerchiefs and the sometimes-calloused palms of their husbands.

Sometimes she daydreamed about what she might have been named. An answer always eluded her, but she knew in her heart that her mother would have given her a name that was pretty. 'Bacac' (the cripple), the unkindest of the nuns called her, other than that she was just a number that nobody wanted.

Here in the village she was just known as the Kelly's girl or that girl up in Kelly's place. Nobody had a first name for her, and it was something that she longed for. The final proof that her existence meant something. That there was a purpose for her life. That she was wanted.

Her hair was her only real asset. Thick and luxurious now, but when she'd first come to this place, she'd been like a badly shorn sheep. Now it was waist length and was her only homage to vanity. She often thought that her mother might have had hair like that. Depending on the light it could change from golden copper to flame-red to the co-lour of ripe yellow corn. It was her hair that brought her to the attention of the man in the black suit.

She remembered the day he came, at the invitation of the nuns, to instruct the older girls for the confirmation. Was it twelve she was at that time or maybe thirteen? She didn't know, certainly no older?

She hadn't liked the way he'd looked at her, like a cat stalking a mouse, weighing up the options, waiting to pounce. The stale smell of tobacco and alcohol off his breath, coupled with his lank greasy hair and the dandruff like slate grey snowflakes on the shoulders and collar of his black coat, she found repulsive. She could never say out loud that she hadn't wanted to take the class, the punish-ment would have been severe for such wickedness.

The man in the black suit preached love and understand-ing, but when he looked at her, the eyes beneath the straight black line of his brows betrayed his words.

Extra tuition was needed he informed the nuns. The girl was stupid, bothering on insolent, and would have to be brought to the parochial house for correction.

On the following Sunday after breakfast, and before mass, a nun scrubbed her with carbolic soap until her skin was raw. The stench of the soap in her nostrils made her want to retch. The nun kept telling her what an honour it was to be privately tutored by the great man in his house. When she protested, she was backhanded across the face, and called the spawn of Satan.

The nun drank tea in the kitchen with the housekeeper, while the black-garbed man led her by the hand to the parlour.

She'd never heard of any religion like his first lesson. Why did he have to put his hands with the filthy nicotine stained fingernails under her clothes? She took the liberty of asking, but he couldn't answer; his face had turned a puce-purple colour, and his breath was coming in short semi-strangled gasps.

The second lesson he had hurt her, hurt her badly. She'd been shocked when she'd bled, staring in horror at the bright crimson stain on her thighs. He'd told her she was saved now, and she should thank him for it. The demons were finally driven out, the blood merely proof of their demise. Every other time it would be easier. There never was another time.

That was the day the Kelly's arrived looking for a child to share their lives and their home. A smallholding in the foothills of the mountains, a long way towards the west.

Her legs tottered beneath her as she was being led back to the orphanage. The shame of her ordeal more painful than the physical abuse.

The couple had just arrived. They'd sat high up in the maroon and gold trap, that was hitched to a shaggy haired piebald pony. The woman had a brightly coloured tartan rug across her knees. The afternoon sun was at their backs, glinting off the polished brass on the pony's harness and the gold painted stripes on the wheels of the trap She had to squint and put one hand across her eyes to look up at a pleasant looking couple that smiled down on her.

When they spoke her heart soared, and she knew with a gut instinct that they'd been sent in answer to her prayers. They were the first strangers that had ever spoken to her. She savoured their words in her mind. Freedom was a stone's throw away.

They were shown all the prime candidates first. No good. Mrs. Kelly was adamant, she wanted girl she'd spoken to on the avenue. The girl with the red hair. They were confused at first not knowing whom she meant, but eventually she was brought down. An hour later she sat between the couple, a small white flour sack filled with her few possessions on her lap clutched as if in the grip of death. The man flicked the whip lightly and the pony leant into the harness taking the strain. The trap moved off. They took the road towards the west. Heading into the sunset behind the clip-clopping hooves of the old pony. As they reached the turn of the road, she took a last look at the dwelling of the priest. It was silhouetted stark black against the deep blood red of the sun, and it seemed to her for a moment that she was looking into the abyss of hell. A hell whose gates had reopened after all these years.

There had been great excitement in the village when word had spread about the coming of a new priest. He was an important man, they said. Someone who had the ear of the bishop. The housekeeper was the one with the news, and for a few days her status was elevated to far above her station. Most of the women in the village had brought flowers to decorate the church for Sunday. There would be a big attendance for his first mass.

On Saturday night at eight o'clock he was hearing confessions. The church would have been thronged to capacity, but being harvest time the men, along with the older boys were still in the fields. The old woman insisted that she attended.

For as long as she'd been in this place, she'd kept her

silence. Never confessed, never told a living soul. It was her secret and she'd take it to the grave. It came her turn. She entered the box, waiting as her eyes grew accustomed to the gloom.

The shutter opened suddenly, and she found herself staring into the face of the devil. She ran from the confessional, ran from the church, and never went back. It was a small place, and an action like hers gave rise to gossip.

They'd questioned her, both of them, but she kept silent. Who would be believed, the cripple or the man in the black suit? If she'd talked, she wondered would it have been any different? She didn't think so.

She stayed away from the church after that. It made her the talk of the place, and she knew the old people were hurt by her actions. It was just a shame that the church couldn't stay away from her.

Every Sunday after mass the priest was invited back to one of the parishioner's houses for breakfast. She knew it had to happen, it eventually got to be the turn of the Kelly's. She avoided eye contact with him and all through the meal ate as if her life depended on it. When she got a chance, she excused herself and left.

It being Sunday she was free until evening milking. She was in the barn when she saw him and knew he was coming for her. He took her there, on top of a pile of empty corn sacks, hurting her and not caring. He just rutted with her like an animal, before emptying himself like a dog into a bitch.

There were no words of love or affection; it was just an act to gratify his basic cravings. She had once heard the old woman say that people are known by their deeds, if that was so then this man was incapable of showing real love or affection to anyone.

That had been three months ago. He'd come back many times since, always making demands, unholy demands. The only certainty being he always hurt her.

She looked down at her thickening waist. She knew the old woman suspected that things weren't as they should be. She'd been sick in the mornings and her mother had heard her. She didn't want to hurt them. They were kind people and had been good to her in so far as they were able. They were the only ones that had ever shown her love, and was this to be how she repaid them? They wouldn't deserve the grief and shame that knowledge of her condition would heap on them.

The light was fading fast and the last pink rays of the sun were just visible through the skylight glass.

She brushed her hair and put on her blouse and skirt, the ones she kept for Sunday. Her shoes she polished with an old bacon bone. Polished until her reflection stared back at her from the gleaming black leather. Finally she took down her good coat from the hook behind the door, then sat on the bed and waited.

At last she heard the muted music from the old radio fading and dying. The scrape and rattle of the fire irons as Mattie banked the fire and added a few sods of turf. The creak of the bed springs as the old pair settled for the night, then silence. Silence; disturbed only by the scratching of mice and the hiss of flames from the burning turf.

It was fully dark as she descended the ladder, moving carefully and as silently as possible. The third rung from the bottom creaked, so she stretched herself to avoid that.

In the kitchen she stood listening. Only deep breathing and muffled snoring. The old couple were asleep.

She left the house by the backdoor, fearful of the creaking of the hinges or the screech of the bolt. The dog was lying by the gate of the yard. He stood as she passed, wagging his tail. She stooped for a minute to stroke his head. He followed her as far as the road, then stood watching as she walked towards the village. At the creamery, she stopped by the bridge and stood for a long time gazing into the dark swirling water.

She marvelled at the reflection of the moon, and how the stars seemed to dance with the ripples. Her unborn baby she named for the old man. Matthew, named for the finest man she could ever have imagined knowing. She was sure it would be a boy, and he'd like that. A hawk hovered high overhead, silhouetted against the silver of the moon his wingspan spread like those of an angel. It really was a beautiful night, a silent night. An almost imperceptible splash as if a fish had broken the surface of the water was the only sound to intrude into the stillness.

The following Sunday in the church, the man in the black suit stood on the altar. He was pleading forgiveness and salvation for the girl who by her wanton wickedness had flown in the face of the Almighty. A girl who had chosen to end her life in such a cowardly manner. The tongue of the serpent wove a tapestry of eloquence. The Kelly's did not attend.

A few days later, the river gave back what it had been given. The snow-white corpse of the girl.

This time the old couple sat in the front pew. She rested her head on the shoulder of her husband, tears streaming down her weather-beaten face. The face of a woman with a broken heart. In one hand she held a worn rosary beads, in the other a grubby tear-stained handkerchief. The old man sat with one arm around her. Holding her, comforting her, wishing he could lift the burden of pain from her bone-thin shoulders.

The plain pine-board coffin lay on wooden trestles before the altar. The girl they'd always thought of as their daughter was in that coffin. She hadn't taken her own life, she wasn't that kind. It had been taken from her. That was murder wasn't it?

The prayers were said by a younger priest, a distant relation of Maeve's, brought in for the occasion. He tried his best, but for the words to be sincere they would have to be spoken by someone that meant them. Someone that had known the girl. Mattie didn't hear them. He wasn't listening.

The murmured responses filled the church with a low hum, almost as if a hive was swarming. The shoulders of the old woman heaved as the sobs racked her thin frame. She buried her face against the sleeve of his coat, trying to muffle the sounds of her sorrow.

He remembered her excitement when they'd first seen the girl on the avenue leading to the orphanage. Her faltering steps like those of a new-born foal as she tottered by them on her thin legs. How proud she was as the adoption papers were signed. They'd been given a daughter. The girl was going home with them. Their prayers had been answered. Dreams did come true.

Dreams that would now only be the rambling imaginings of an old couple. Dreams that would never now be fulfilled. They would never know the joy of dancing at their daughter's wedding. They'd never now sit beneath the shade of the apple trees and watch their grandchildren play hide-and-seek in the haggard or hear the happy sound of their laughter filling the empty spaces in their lives.

The voice from the altar droned on, beseeching God's forgiveness for the misguided actions of the girl.

Bile rose in his throat, nauseating him. The girl was innocent. What had she done that required forgiveness?

He looked around at the faces of the congregation. It seemed to him that every eye in the church seemed to stare back at him. He met all of their eyes squarely, full on, no one looked away. These were his friends, his people, here to support himself and his wife in their hour of need. He knew them all, each and every one, as he'd known their fathers before them. In the time that the girl had been missing these were the people that had selflessly put their own lives on hold to lend their support in any way they could. They were from both sides of the religious divide, but today differences were laid aside. The one religion they all shared was their respect for each other.

They were good people. They had come from the neighbouring villages. Some had come from across the mountain. They were here because they understood his sorrow, felt his pain, and shared his grief.

At that moment Matthew Kelly swore an oath that his girl would be avenged. He squeezed the hand of the old woman gently and looked around once more at the faces behind him. He appraised them, from the teary-eyed faces of the women to the stoic features of the men. The die was cast. The decision made.

The praying was done. They hadn't wanted any hymns.

Just a verse or two of an old ballad she'd once been given by the tinker. It was the song the girl liked best. One of the village women began the verse, others joined her.

'All around my hat I will wear a green willow,
all around my hat until death comes...'

The voices were lost as the church bell tolled. He thought it the most lonesome sound he'd ever heard. The coffin was shouldered from the church.

Mattie looked at the house of the priest. From an upstairs window a curtain twitched. Through the salty wetness in his rheumy old eyes he looked at a face that appeared to him to be pitiless. It was a face devoid of mercy, remorseless. A face that carried no trace of guilt or shame. It was the face of evil. The face of the man in the black suit.

The calloused fingers of his right hand caressed the brass caps of the two cartridges he'd chosen especially that morning.

The Town I Once Knew Well
Danny's train Don't Stop Here Anymore

Time is the one great constant in our lives. As it marches on relentlessly it inevitably brings changes in its passing. In my own time, I've seen quite a few changes, but who amongst us hasn't?

I'm a native of Midleton in East Cork. It was a time when doors stood open all day during the daylight hours. When the people next door, were those who could be called on in times of crisis, and not interfering old busybodys.

The bare necessities were all most people had. Though luxuries were rare and foreign holidays unheard of, but somethings never change. The trait of two-pence looking down on a penny was found just as much back then as it is today.

Back in those days of the late fifties and early sixties Midleton was a market town of some significance. It had two large industries. Midleton Worsted Mills and Woolcombers Ltd., collectively known far and wide as The Factory.

Another big employer Erin Foods located on the North side of town, came much later. There, peas from the whole of East Cork and West Waterford were processed. Very few were left without employment during the pea-harvesting season. Huge cold storage facilities were set up and brought in their wake the meat processing plants. There were spin-offs from all these industries for those with a modicum of business acumen and the will to follow a goal. It was a time of opportunity. Midleton at that time was thriving.

We lived in the area known as Knockgriffin, which was the only estate of houses built by the County Council on the Cork side of the town. By the standards of today it would be tiny. Just four blocks of six houses with a garden front and back.

Houses 13-24 looked out over what used to be the first golf course in East Cork. By 1960 it had long fallen into disuse, as golf in no way enjoyed the popularity it does today.

The only two people I ever remember swinging a club in that field were local business man Eddie Moriarty and Mr. St.Clair-Rice a solicitor in the town. Eddie was well known in the commercial world. He'd once had a great moment of fame when he designed a pair of boots for a female celebrity, he'd met on a flight to somewhere. Always a gentleman, in my opinion, Eddie was a man light years ahead of his time.

When school was out, that field was our playground. At that time the old bunkers were all still in existence and our playing area covered forty acres. Here, for hours on end boys could ride imaginary horses across the plains of Texas and the badlands of Arizona. Forts were built and we took turns at being either cowboys or Indians.

Quite a large pond that at one time might have been a water trap provided us with a readymade sea on which to sail our bits of wood, (aka) pirate ships in search of treasure. We never found any, but the fun we had in trying was priceless.

The lower end of the field was bounded by the Owenacurra river before it joined the tidal water further out below the town and was the first place we all paddled and the bravest among us took the plunge and learned to swim.

On Sunday evenings it was matinee time at the Or-
monde cinema on the Coolbawn. First stop was Moore's
shop where the most delicious ice cream was sold, bicycles
could be left in safety and when a jukebox was installed, we
thought it was teenage heaven.

In the cinema for two hours on a Sunday evening our
heroes controlled our lives. Audie Murphy went 'To Hell
and Back'. Tumbleweeds blew across the prairies and we
dodged bullets by the O.K Corral as the legends of the Wild
West came to life before our eyes.

Young Danny from No. 23 was a boy gifted with an
imagination only few are blessed with. Danny's train was
his forte. It wasn't a real train, it was just Danny. Every
evening after school he'd run a circuit of the twenty-four
houses, stopping at each front gate with squeal of brakes
and the hiss of steam. He'd imitate all the sounds a real
train might make. The train had a schedule and ran to time.
Any kids with a few pennies to spend would on hearing the
'whoooooo whooooo' of the train whistle, jump on Danny's wonderful imaginary train to be carried to Moriarty's
shop on the corner. My sister Rita was a regular commuter.
She always travelled by train.

I can say without fear of contradiction that in No.7 lived
a boy that fate in its wisdom destined for greatness. Someone
who by his prowess on the field of sport put Midleton, and
more especially Cork, into the sporting chronicles on more
than one occasion. John Fenton was a titan on the hurling
field and a stalwart of the Cork team on many occasions.

Since he was old enough to hold a hurley he gave the
sport his all. Before school every morning and every evening John was in the field hitting that ball. Weather was of

no consequence; rain or shine the game went on, he chased that ball and scored.

Since its inception no one ever involved with hurling ever had the dedication or focus of John Fenton. He wore the red jersey of Cork with pride and earned his place in the annals of the G.A.A with an unsurpassed distinction. Who will ever forget that day in Thurles 1987? The day John scored from the halfway line, a goal that never has, or won't ever be equalled.

The Limerick keeper had no chance, none at all. The blend of dynamics coupled with the skill of John Fenton could only be described as poetry. In the space of a heart-beat the ball was in the net and he had scored what was without a doubt the goal of a lifetime.

When East Cork men talk of hurling John Fenton can stand beside the best. He left a legacy that will never be forgotten. He's a role model that can only always be held in the highest esteem, a true hero, and always a modest and unassuming gentleman.

Jimmy Glavin and his horse delivered the coal from Sutton's yard on the Coolbawn around our terrace. He was in every sense of the word a gentleman of the old school and the first man I remember thinking was really strong. His face was round; shiny as a full moon and his hair appeared to have been dipped in silver. Habitually a bandana that could have been any colour, but was always black from coal-dust was knotted at his throat. He always wore a shirt with no collar beneath a waistcoat that would have been the third part of a suit, and corduroy trousers with the legs tied above the knee with bits of string. His leather boots had so many steel studs in the soles it was amazing he was able to lift them.

A polite tap on the back door announced his arrival. The woman of the house was always addressed as ma'am, and the man called by his first name. After a few polite words of chat, he'd get his order and carry the sack of coal in on his shoulder.

The kids on the road loved to feed the horse. More often than not it was just fistfuls of grass, but every now and again an apple or a carrot was filched from the kitchen cupboard. We called each other names, wrestled and at times noses were bloodied over who should have the honour to be first to feed the horse. Progress raised an ugly head in the form of mechanised transport. The horse was retired, and the very affable Jimmy relegated to the coal yard.

In the days before pasteurisation milk was delivered every morning fresh from the cows on Beecher's farm. The chestnut pony pulled the milk float around the terraces, the housewives brought their jugs, and the full cream milk was dispensed from the big shiny churns.

On Tuesday at 12 o'clock the travelling shop came by. Driven by a local Cork Road man Eddie Hayes, every conceivable item was stocked, and it provided an invaluable service.

In the early sixties, television was transmitted for the first time to the East Cork region. The pictures were often so grainy as to be at times almost indecipherable, but it brought a hitherto unknown world into people's homes.

Billy Ramsell was a character without peer. His family lived at No.16 and had the first television in the terraces. At the time 'The Fugitive' was without doubt the first big serial to catch the public's imagination. On the nights it was on people crowded into Ramsell's sitting room. Everyone wanted to see the hunt for the 'one-armed man'. It didn't matter if she knew them or not, Annie Ramsell despite having a big family of her own, never turned anyone away. The front window was left open so the waiting hoards in the garden could have the story relayed to them by the gobsmacked audience squashed around the television set. On more than one occasion sightings of the elusive 'one-armed man' were reported to the local guards by the imaginative, but very naïve viewers.

It was kids night in Ramsell's when JFK was shot in Dallas. Mrs. Ramsell was left to break the bad news, all programs were cancelled for the night. When realisation took hold, kids broke down in tears. The scene was catastrophic. Didn't JFK know what night it was? Obviously not as Jack Lord (aka) Stony Burke, bronco rider left the rodeo ring and faded from the screen.

These people were the salt of the earth. If you were someone's neighbour it meant a great deal more than just living next door, you shared their lives.

On the Cork side of the town where the bridge spans the river, was where the Sons of Rest held sway. A local myth and tongue-in-cheek explanation for the name was that if work was available the 'Sons' had the uncanny ability to be somewhere else and thus avoided it.

I thought at the time that they were all quite old men, but they weren't really, just a lot older than I was. They all had nicknames and I suspect a few had forgotten what they were originally christened. The names were legion, Spider, Soapy Water, Dodo, Coaxie, Jack the Belcher, Coachman, Balls of Twine, Tack, Gachee, Daz… the list is endless.

On a seat by the bridge three or four of these guardians of leisure, like elder statesmen would hold court daily. Invariably, tied to the seat with a piece of twine were a brace of mongrels. Like sentinels guarding the entrance to their territory nothing that crossed the bridge escaped the scrutiny of the watchers. Everyone who passed was fair game to be commented on by the 'Sons'. The flat-capped men shared a pouch of tobacco and sat in judgement. This was their oyster, and they were more than happy to let the world pass them by.

When the 'Tans' sought to control East Cork, they would have had to cross that bridge. The inscrutable eyes of the guardians would have noted their comings and watched their going.

The green triangle known locally as The Goose's Acre was at the top end of the Main St. where the road forked north towards Fermoy and swung westwards towards Cork city. In bygone days it was commonage, where according to legend a local woman, Kate Barry grazed her gaggle of geese.

A large limestone trough stood at one side where visitors to the town could water their horses beneath elms, sycamores and horse chestnuts. The green was idyllic, a focal point and a source of pride to the people of the area.

Alas it no longer exists, a front-line faller in the race for progress, Perhaps Ray Lawton, local raconteur and wit (now sadly deceased) best expressed the fate that befell the green with these few lines.

'They hanged the felon who stole the goose from out the acre, but let the greater felons loose, who stole the acre from the goose'.

Looking back on it now, it was a no bad time to grow up. Things were done differently and at a pace to suit everybody. Anna Barry and her sisters Eily and Kitty sold biscuits and sweets in their small grocery shop on the Cork road. The measures were generous, and Coca-Cola was still the real thing.

I remember Patsy O'Connell's grocery and bar. The top shelves of the shop stacked with a huge variety of Jacob's biscuits in large square tins. Kimberly, Mikado, Fig Rolls, Coconut Creams, Rich Tea, Chocolate Digestives, Ginger Nuts. Looking through the eyes of a small boy; mouth- watering stuff.

On Saturday morning women lined the counter to pay off the credit of the previous week. Anyone with an account not in arrears got a discount of sixpence in the pound. Where would you get a deal like that today?

The main street of that town had everything. You name it, Midleton provided it. Butchers, bakers, shoe shops, barbers, hairdressers, hardware, pubs, restaurants and even a fish and chip shop. Times changed. Some survived, most did not.

What is now the Post Office was once the grocery and public house of Dick Barry. The premises was a long narrow shop, with a bar at the back. Dick was a charismatic type of character who always had a smile and a cheerful word for any passer-by. Always a sharp dresser, he never appeared without a handkerchief in his breast pocket and a carnation in his buttonhole. He always gave the impression of someone that might have been a leading man in an old-time movie and had just stepped off the silver screen.

A gleaming stainless steel 'Berkley' meat slicing machine

stood on the counter-top, alongside a large roll of brown wrapping paper, a commodity much sought after at the time. In the post-war years, not long after rationing finished, It was predicted that a time would come when brown paper would have more value than gold. Standing by the wall of the small office was a large brass-topped machine, used for the grinding of coffee beans. The aroma of freshly ground coffee from those by-gone days still lingers in my memory, but for me, the real thing is not around anymore.

Butter, fresh from Leahy's farm at East Ferry, was wrapped in greaseproof paper and sold in pound and half-pound slabs. Thick and creamy, the colour of sunlight on daffodils, it tasted divine.

The bar was a fascinating place to me. On a cold evening in winter, with the large pot-bellied stove glowing red on the black flagstone floor, it was a place to be. For an arm-rest a gleaming brass rail ran the length of the counter top, well- polished by the elbows of the thirsty.

From cattle drovers to doctors, teachers to solicitors, the greatest cross-section of characters from all walks of life frequented that bar. The tales told by and about them was an education not to be got in any school classroom.

At the corner of Connelly St. on a Friday, Tommy Sliney from Ballycotton, sold fish from the back of his donkey and cart. When Tommy retired, local man Tommy Conners took over the pitch. Great men and characters. It was a place and a way of life, gone now, and unfortunately lost forever.

Midleton is now a huge town. Much bigger than most, it's a sprawling mass of housing estates spreading out to all points of the compass. The railway station has been refurbished and the Cork-Midleton rail-link restored after decades of disuse. In many aspects it would seem to be a thriving place, but the big employers have all departed.

For most people the days of having full employment are now just distant memories. The main offices of 'The Factory' a place that once employed people in their hundreds, still has thousands going through those self-same doors. Sad to say it's no longer to work, but to sign on. A place where people once collected their wages is now, a few short years later, a place where people are processed for benefits. It's a sad indictment of the times.

'Don't worry,' we're told. 'Live with it, it's all about progress ...

It's the way thing are now.' That doesn't mean it should hang right with me. Maybe it's the way I am, but I find I'm continually running against the wind, floundering in a flood tide, the water getting deeper all the time. The only thing that doesn't change fast enough is my mind.

Lately I sat waiting for a friend on the steps of what used to be the town hall, now it's the library. Two girls, rather women in their late twenties, sat nearby. They were busy, no talk, just fingers twitching on the keypads of phones. Busy as they texted their conversation to each other. How sad was that?

I stood on the bridge where the old men used to sit. The seat is no longer there. Though I scarcely knew them, I miss them, as one would miss long departed friends. There was nothing to show that they'd ever existed, but their ghosts.

The wind blew across the road from where long ago, Kate Barry's geese grazed the acre. The wind blew changes, bringing acceptance that the town has changed and life as I knew it has gone forever. I caught a glimpse of the new commuter train as it glided by, smooth and silent as it passed what had once been the food plant.

There was no whistle. Danny's train don't stop here anymore.

...Of all the Bloody Days ...

(Diary of an Accident)

Wednesday, 13th December 2015

Bang! I was afraid to look at my hand, instead I searched the floor for my fingers. I didn't feel the pain, but I did see the blood. Buckets of it. Sprayed across the ceiling and running down the walls.

Oh Sweet Jesus! What the f*** do I do now?

Help was needed. Sooner rather than later. Panic button wasn't working. Where the hell was my phone? Coat pockets? No. Under cushions? No. The last place I looked, right where I always leave it. Who to call?

Panic was setting in. My dogs were looking up at me, concern etched on their faces. There was so much blood, I'd visions of bleeding out before help arrived. I called my friend. A man whom I knew could be depended on in a crisis. Sometimes miracles do happen. This was one of such occasion. My friend and his wife were passing my gate. Within a minute they were at the door.

The Health Centre was reached in double quick time. Luckily I met my own G.P. on the way to lunch. He rushed me to surgery and called for back-up. Washed clean, disinfected and examined, the conclusion was, that I'd have to go further. With the wounded fingers dressed, they armed me with antibiotics, and a copious amount of pain-killers. I was then issued with orders to check into the Plastic Surgery Clinic in Cork the following morning.

Thursday 14th December 2015

Amazing how a handful of pain killers and a half-pint of Jamesons can have such a stunning effect. Well rested, I was abroad early. Myself and my travelling companions, Twister and Buddy were at our destination an hour before time.

Great, I was first in the queue. I needed to be. At that stage, my bandage looked like a blood-soaked sponge. I waited. The appointment time of 9 o'clock came. Then, it went again. At 9.30, a lady started taking details.

How long will it be? I've no idea, just take a seat and wait your turn.

A nurse arrived.9.40. No sign of a doctor. I waited some more. Swish, swish, swishing sound in the corridor. Same sound entered waiting room and swished right on by me. Yippee! Her Majesty had condescended to grant an audience to the impaired. It had just turned 9.50. The swish, swish, swishing noise? She was wearing a pair of hospital issue trousers. The legs at least six-inches too long. She must have been a busy woman, as turning up a hem hadn't bothered her. She didn't bother to close the door between the waiting room and the dressing clinic either. Fascinated, I watched, as this unexpected insight into the daily doings of a Health Care professional, unfolded before me.

First order of the day. Madame dispatched the nurse to fetch a take-away coffee. Red-faced, with eyes averted, the nurse scurried past the waiting queue. Every sip of the chosen beverage was savoured at her Ladyship's leisure. In the waiting room, a child started howling. At last, action. The nurse informed us pilgrims, that the children would be seen to first. Fair enough. There were two of them. I was next.

Eventually, at just turned eleven, I was called. The nurse, very efficiently, took off the dressing. The eyes of the H.S.E professional looked at my injuries from a distance of five feet.

Has this been x-rayed? No! Typical, that should have been done before you came here. Get it done now. Where? The x-ray department.

I was dismissed. I made my way down a mile of corridor to the x-ray room. There I joined another queue. Not too bad. It only took an hour. Back in the original outpost, I found I'd lost my place. There was now four ahead of me. Five minutes later the nurse, called my name. Great. Was I next?

Was I hell. Return to X-ray Dept. Some technical hitch.

Back I went. The technical hitch? The introductory note I'd been given, had been mostly illegible. They'd only shot two fingers instead of three. So much for doctor's hand-writing.

Back again, just one waiting this time. Ten minutes later, the Eye's of the Almighty, studied the x-rays. Upside down, inside out and sideways. Over the shoulder, instructions were issued to the nurse.

Nothing broken, fingers just need dressing. Make out a prescription for blah, blah, blah...

A different nurse this time. A cheerful, chatty woman, from the Cork-Kerry border told me laughingly, that dressings weren't her strongest suite. Not a woman that told lies. By the time she'd finished wrapping yards of bandage around my fingers, they closely resembled Pinnochio's nose.

There was no talk of a return visit. I didn't care. I was out of there. The time? Three o'clock.

Friday 15th December 2015

Seven o'clock. The phone rings. Surprise surprise. None other than the Empress of Plastic Surgery. I was honoured.

Wait on a phone call tomorrow for a time to revisit. Morning or evening? You'll be told that, but you will be seen tomorrow. Good-bye.

Saturday 16th December 2015

Nothing like being ready. My dogs and myself were abroad at 6 am, and on the road to Midleton. My friend was going to mind them for the day. I waited. All day long I waited. That promised phone call never came. By late evening, despite the tablets, the pain was driving me insane.

Sunday 17th December 2015

Sunday morning, I knew I was in dire straits. I phoned local hospital. Very sympathetic lady on the switchboard, re-directed me to someone in authority.

'We're very sorry sir, but the government has closed our A&E. The Dressing Clinic is only operating Monday to Friday.'

Feck! Don't get injured at weekends. What should I do?

'Try South Doc. They may be able to help.'

I followed the instructions. At 10 a.m. I checked into South Doc. Great. I was seen immediately. The doctor peeled off the (by now filthy bandage) and grimaced.

That's nasty, very nasty. I'm sorry, but I'm not touching it. You'll have to go back to the hospital. Not tomorrow, today. If it's not attended to within a few hours, it might well be too late. All three fingers are badly infected.'

He re-dressed the injuries and gave me a letter.

At 11.15 I was back in the same clinic I'd attended on Thursday. Three doctors names, on the duty roster. Nobody about. I waited. At 1.30 I went to get a drink from the machine and returned to my place. I asked a passing member of the cleaning staff did anyone work on Sundays? In broad Indonesian, or some such accent, she answered.

'Yes, No! I've no idea where everybody is. I expect they're busy elsewhere.'

At 1.45 a nurse arrived. I explained my predicament. I think she'd heard it all before.

'I don't think you'll be seen today. All the doctors are in theatre.'

I was waiting so long. I thought they must have gone to the Christmas Pantomime.

'Can you wait? If no one comes by 2.30 I'll make a phone call.'

It wasn't as if I'd anything else to do. I waited. The nurse returned and made the phone call.

'I'm very sorry, but it's as I said. You won't be seen today. You're to go home and wait for a phone call.'

I'd been down that road, it was never going to happen. I tried explaining what The South Doc medic had told me.

'He's probably exaggerating. Doctors are quite fond of erring on the side of caution.'

As diplomatically as I could, but with blood pressure rising, I laid out the scenario as I saw it. I wasn't going anywhere until my hand was seen to.

'Wait until 3.30, then I'll phone again. Have you eaten?'

To give the woman her due, she went off, and returned with a very welcome ham sandwich and a mug of tea. At 3.30 she called again. The answer received was the same as previously.

'I'll dress your hand before you go home.'

For the second time that day, the bandages came off. My hand smelled like a rotting corpse. The nurse ran to the phone.

'This man can't be left home, his hand is too badly infected. It's smelling really badly. He'll be seen this evening? Okay, I'll tell him that.'

The nurse departed. Five minutes later she returned, bearing another ham sandwich and a mug of tea. At 5.10 I heard again the swish, swish, swishing sound. No prize for guessing who entered. She never spoke, or made eye contact. Just went to sit in the corner and fiddled with her phone. I had the measure of her then. Talk about having egg on the face. This woman, had just been given a serious dressing down. Seconds later an Indian lady arrived. The others jumped to attention when she entered. Young, well dressed, and seemingly in charge, she introduced herself, as the senior surgeon on the shift.

'You've a very serious injury, Mr. Stack. Tell me the whole story, beginning to end. It's important you leave nothing out'.

If revenge is a dish best served cold, then I gave it everything I had. If a certain party had been hung out to dry, she'd brought it on herself. I could see the Indian lady was appalled. Anger crackled in every word and gesture, as she ordered Dr. Muppet about.

My hand was treated. The Indian woman worked quickly and efficiently. Within minutes I'd received eight shots of anistethic. With a scalpel, she removed all infected matter. Then, the fingers, I was told on Thursday only needed dressing, received twenty-eight stitches in total. Then, this very efficient lady, instructed the nurse, to schedule all return appointments for times, when she herself would be working in the dressing clinic. I think that woman may well have been my Guardian Angel.

The Outcome. Mid-Feburary 2016

If I'd sat at home, waiting on a phone-call, the outcome would have been entirely different. For the nursing staff of the hospital I've nothing but the higest regard. They work hard, under the most difficult conditions. I can't say the same for the attitude of the first surgeon that attended me. I took into consideration she might have been having a bad day. We all have them. I could make allowances for that. On return visits, having observed her from a distance, I can say, hand on heart, I was reading her right first time.

All in all, I was more than a little lucky. Thankfully I had good result, from an extremely bad experience.

Today I Bought a Smartphone

The bane of my life

I f anyone is expecting a call from me, don't hold your breath. It probably won't happen. Why? You may well ask.

A few days ago I decided, that for me, the age of the dinosaur had come to an end. I embraced the heart of modern-day technology and bought myself a Smart-phone.

Not, I assure you, a decision made lightly. For weeks I browsed web-sites, read reviews and went through every possible combination of pros and cons. Did I know phones inside out? No! I thought I did.

So, Smart-Phone. My first one and what can I say? The feckin' thing is way too smart for me. I had seventy-seven contacts. Had 'em for years and never had a problem. What happens? On Saturday I try to make a call and just like that, I ended up killing forty-two. Yes! You heard me right. Forty-two friends and aquaintences came to an untimely end. I pressed a button and annililated people I've known for years. Blasted them into cyber-space with my newly acquired deadly weapon, a Samsung J3.

My God! There were good men in there. Men with families, woman with kids, some of my grandchildren, my own three kids. It didn't matter. Samsung a deadly song. It made no distinction, took no prisoners. Quite mercilessy, it killed them all.

I sat there stunned. Tesco's car-park was like a battle ground. Bodies strewn everywhere. What to do? Panic.

That's what I did. I shot out of that parking space, wheels spinning and headed for the motor-way. I drove carefully, heart beating louder than an Orangeman's drum. Checking speed and rear-view mirror, waiting for those flashing blue lights to close in on me. Nothing. Surely someone must have noticed.

No! An hour later, I crawled towards my house. All was quiet. I turned on the six o'clock news. It didn't even warrant a mention. W. T. F. was happening? Had everyone gone blind? Here I was, comfortable in my armchair, a dog's head resting on each knee and no one, but no one, seems to give a damn that there's a killer on the loose.

That night, in a skirmish in the garden, I took out ten more. The following morning, wearing dark glasses and a hoodie, I bought the paper. Surely I'd be headline news. Not as much as a by-line, not to mention a headline.

I went back for another look. The car-park was empty. Some phone company gopher must have removed the evidence. Nothing to be seen. They hadn't even put my pic up on the police station notice board. Didn't anyone want to know? 'Here I am! Look at me!' I felt like shouting. 'I'm a killer on the loose.'

Phew! Waste of time and thought. Nobody gave me a second glance, nobody cared. I believe nobody even saw me. They wandered passed as if comatosed, eyes glued to Smart-phones.

Me? Right now, that damn phone is at one side of the room, I'm at the other. Eyes locked, that unblinking selfie lens is staring straight at me. There's no compromise. This is war. 'Come on you bastard!' I hear myself screaming. 'Do your worst. Ring now you idiot. I dare you. Make my day.'

The Smart-phone lives up to its name. Lounging casually on the sofa, dressed in its gleaming silver suit, it just stares back at me. Dignified, it remains calmly aloof and menacingly silent.

Dead on Time

Valentines Night... Oh God! That's what happened!

Detective-Sergeant Shannon Waters opened one eye and tentatively extended a hand, probing beneath the rumpled duvet. Searching... Suddenly she was wide awake. The opposite side of the king-size bed was empty.

OMG! What had happened? Her head hurt and one eye seemed to have developed an uncontrollable twitch. Oh God! She grabbed a pillow and hugged it. Where the hell was she?

Slowly. Very slowly, like snow melting after a cold snap, the truth, in isolated patches began to be exposed. Half-way through her thawing disbelief, a vague outline of the story was starting to take shape. It would take coffee, black, un-sweetened and lots of it, before the negative images of the jigsaw she'd uncovered, formed into a full colour picture of the truth.

Ohooooo! She let out a long drawn out groan of what might have been pain, but was more than likely self-pity. Last night?

Valentines night... Oh God! That's what happened.

The pieces started to drift together. Most were still swirling about, but a few were clicking into place. It was not a pretty picture.

Before the clock started ticking towards going home time It had been a hectic, all hands to the mops, type of day at the station. The window fans were battling to clear the last of the day's cigarette smoke, when the phone call had come.

She'd heard what was said, but at first, hadn't believed it. Then she did. It started to make sense. It was a young woman. Anonymous as they always are, she'd thought. The woman sounded panic stricken. Somewhere in the background a child was bawling. The voice of another, older child, was shouting at her mother to do something.

She'd scribbled down an address. 'Yes, yes, of course I'll be there. Talk to no one else. Tomorrow morning, ten o'clock sharp. Thanks.' Before she could say goodbye, the line went silent.

She'd scrolled through the call log. Put the number in her phone and deleted the recording. Extremely unethical and decidedly foolish, but when needs must...? Then she'd pulled the scribbled address from the notepad and put it in the tiny watch pocket of her trousers.

Whew! She let out a long sigh of relief. Things might not be so bad after all. Only a few pieces of the puzzle left. Just some questions needed answering. Where was she? How did she get here and who with? Most importantly what the blazes had she been doing? She threw back the duvet cover.

Oh! My God! This can't be happening. Now! *Where the bloody hell are my knickers?*

She glanced all around, trying to encompass all areas at once, but the puzzle was a long way short of being completed. She called out. Her voice echoed, sounding hollow and far off. The house was silent. At least she was still wearing her watch.

Not a lot of use, that wouldn't cover much.

Sitting back down on the bed, she checked the time. Not bad, 7.10 February16th.

Whaaaat? That couldn't be right.

Surely it was February 15$^{th.}$ She unclipped the strap and shook the watch. Same result. She banged it off the headboard. The date remained exactly as it had been. What the hell had happened? There was a day missing. Surely someone must have missed her.

She tried to think. Tried to be as logically rational about this situation as she'd been trained to do. Logic provided no answers. The textbooks had somehow failed to mention the solution to waking up in alien surroundings without your knickers.

That something happened was not in doubt, the question was what? She shouldn't have gone in that bar. Alcohol was her problem. She'd been aware that she been bordering on alcholism, the warning sign had been in place a long time, but she'd studiously ignored them.

It was something she'd missed, the atmosphere about the city on Valentine's night.

What harm could one do?

Quite a lot obviously, but easy to be wise after the fact. There had been a guy, tall, friendly, he'd bought the second, she'd called the third. They'd laughed, touched hands even, then the night spiralled out of control. She couldn't focus on his face. That damn fog just wouldn't shift.

How had she got back here. She hadn't an inkling. *Nothing for it. Recover her clothes, explore the property, find out where she was and get the hell out of here. Oh God! Every muscle hurt.*

She padded about, conscious of her state of undress. *'Ouch!'* Oh fuck, that hurt. She'd stubbed her toe. She limped to the on-suite bathroom. Total shock. The place was sterile. The only sign that anyone might ever have been in there was a half-used roll of toilet paper. Mind you, it was scented. Good stuff, as if it mattered. No shower gels, shampoos or deodorants. No razors, soaps or towels.

The rest of the house was similar. No pictures, no furniture, no clothes waiting for an owner to return. There was nothing. The only company she had was her shadow, dark against the stark whiteness of the walls. The kitchen, she left until last.

Success. Her clothes. Scattered about the floor, but everything seemed to be there. She dressed as quickly as it was possible to do. Phone and wallet still in her jacket. First a call to explain her absence. Funny that. No signal. She shook the phone. Nothing. No battery and no sim. Dead as...? Just dead. Anger burst over her. She flung what should have been her lifeline, against the wall.

Water. She needed water. No glasses. She could only gulp and dribble from the kitchen tap until her thirst was sated. Her head was spinning. What in blazes had gone on?

Then she saw the papers displayed on the countertop. Photographs. Computer printouts, in full colour. She ruffled through them, then looked. The bile flooded up her throat and the retching had her running for the kitchen sink. Nausea like a tidal-wave engulfed her. She clutched with fingers of straw to the sink edge for support as her knees turned to jelly.

What seemed like a lifetime later, but was a whole lot less, she came back to the real world. Slumped on the hard, cold tiles, whimpering like an ill-treated pup.

Second time around she forced herself to study the pictures in detail. It didn't get easier, but she looked for clues. There were none. She had been assaulted. That much was portrayed in every graphic image, shot close-up and in colour. Two people. Males. White. No rings, body piercings, tattoos or any identifying marks. No head shots of any of the perps.

Did she do that? She must have. It even looked as if she'd been enjoying it.

There was obviously a video on a hard drive somewhere. Her career was finished. That much was certain. She was going down, so she might as well bow out in a blaze of glory. Close the book on the serial rapist 'The Stiletto Man,' and the kudos could be her epitaph. Etched forever on her gravestone. The thought burned her eyes and caused tears to roll down her cheeks.

Gulping more water, she tried to make sense of her predicament. She'd been drugged. The guy in the bar must have slipped her a 'roofie,' as Rohypnol was known on the streets. At least ten times more potent than Valium, the drug must have been fed to her several times to say she'd lost a day. Nothing else could explain it.

What first? The morning after the morning after pill or get her skates on and do some work. Second choice won. The address she'd been given was still stuffed in her watch pocket. Hurting all over, she managed a shambling stumble to the door and bracing herself, prepared to meet the day.

The road seemed miles away. Every step towards it hurt like hell. Her head felt too heavy for her body and wobbled about so much she thought it might fall off.

The time had turned ten o'clock, but the road was silent. Decision time, right or left? Did it matter? Either direction had to lead somewhere. She turned left.

All around her the scene was the same. Fields, some green, some brown. Trees lined the far horizon, dark against the grey of the sky. Somewhere, from a long way off, a church bell tolled. She trudged on.

Exhausted. When her luck changed, she almost missed the moment.

The car had gone a well past her before it stopped. It reversed erratically to where she squatted by the roadside. Warily, through the open window, she surveyed the occupant. He looked safe. Old enough and every bit as decrepit as his car; besides, he was wearing a dog collar.

She produced her ID badge and the page from the notebook. He nodded. He was going that way. The journey, apart from comments about the weather, was undertaken in silence. The wheels turned. The nausea lifted.

She thanked him for the lift. He muttered some mumbo-jumbo. In Latin? A blessing? Maybe.

Checking the address again, she noted it was a housing estate. Not a very large one. She walked towards the imposing entrance. Impressive houses with large frontages on both sides of a not very long, straight road. Speedbumps for traffic control. Signs stating 'Cul de Sac' and 'Children Crossing.' Easy-peasy. Odd numbers on the left, even on the right. What could be simpler?

Without appearing to observe anything, she passed the house on the opposite sidewalk. Everything looked as it should be. The road was quiet. A kid, wearing the colours of a Premiership team, shouted encouragement to himself as he kicked a brightly coloured ball against a gable wall. At the end, she crossed over and doubled back. At the second house, she rang the doorbell on a pretext of making an enquiry. She received no answer.

The scene had changed. Across the street, a tall man, wearing a red baseball cap and white painter's overalls was on a ladder, cleaning windows. A radio was belting out some old rock-n-roll tune. She reached the right address and turned in the gateway. No bell, the door opened on the third knock.

Not as much as she'd have liked, but it opened. From the narrow aperture, two fear-filled, eyes stared out at her. Somewhere in the background a child was still bawling.

'Hello. I'm Detective-Serg…'

'I don't care if your Ms. 'Bloody' Marple. You should have come yesterday. You'll get me bloody killed. Now go.'

'Not without hearing what you've got to say.'

'Nothing. Not any more I haven't. Now bugger off. I'm being watched. Go on! Get out of here.'

The woman was distraught, on the verge of hysteria. 'Who's? Who's watching?'

'Will you do one. Just fuck off befo…' The sentence went unfinished. The door slammed shut.

Nothing for it. Return to the station, eat humble pie and return with a warrant and back-up. Being a maverick, it wouldn't her first time, but it could be done. She checked the street. The window cleaner had gone.

Thirty minutes later she found a bus stop. The elderly driver flashed a beaming smile at her. Half a minute later she was heading back to where she'd started from two evenings before.

In a window seat towards the rear of the vehicle, she rested her head against the glass, closed her eyes and tried to make sense of the situation. Not easy. The heat through the window was making her drowsy. She tried unsuccessfully to stifle a yawn. So much had happened in so short a time.

At the second next stop, she never noticed a tall man wearing a red base-ball cap, sit directly behind her. She never really noticed anything ever again. Two stops later the man alighted the vehicle. The bus drove on.

Forty minutes later the body of the late Detective-Sergeant Shannon Waters was discovered at the bus depot. Her eyes were wide open in shock as a thin trickle of blood seeped from her open mouth. The single, rear-entry stab wound from double-edged stiletto had pierced her heart. The thin blade pinned her to the seat. The bus was on schedule. She'd arrived. Dead on time.

A Day in the Life...

I fell instantly and enviously in love with them

To all intents and purposes what you're reading may seem to be nothing more than a story about a belt buckle. That's where you'd be so wrong. Sure it's about buckle, but it's not just any buckle. Not to me it isn't. It's a very special buckle and I should know because it's mine. I wear it daily. Have done so for years. I wear it with a great sense of pride and more than a little nostalgia.

Years ago, twenty or so, I was having a drink in a local pub one Sunday afternoon. It was a quiet evening. An elderly man entered and sat beside me. We fell into small-talk conversation as you do. Eventually he turned to me and said. 'Don't take offence lad, but you look to me like a man that would wear a belt buckle.'

I was, I did and I still am. At that time the hair was long and I'd four rings in each ear. Now the hair is gone and the rings reduced to two. Hard times. I showed him my buckle. Big, bold and brass. The word **WELDER** was etched across it. The letters picked out in red Rhinestone.

'Hmmm! 'Interesting,' he said. 'I live just around the corner. Don't move, I'll be back.'

True to his word, five minutes later, he returned. A small box was pushed along the counter. He nodded. I opened it. Inside were about a dozen beautiful buckles. I fell instantly and enviously in love with them.

'I can see you'd be a man to appreciate them,' he said. I want someone to have them that would respect the meaning they have for me.'

He told me the story of each one. Where he'd acquired it and why. Then he told me his story. He'd cancer. Incurable, inoperable. Hadn't long left. He'd moved to the village to be near the sea. I listened and sympathised. The man needed to talk.

He'd been a seaman all his life. Had travelled to places I'd heard of, read about, but would never see. Not in this or probably any other lifetime. He related his stories to me. Tales of shipmates, ships and shipping. Bad companies, great captains.

In the too few hours between between three o'clock and closing time in Ballinacurra village in East Cork, I visited them all. Through those precious hours I looked at the world through the eyes of a softly spoken man from the Northside of Cork city. It was a world light years away from anything I might have imagined.

Freight had been his thing. He'd steamed to all quarters of the globe on every type of vessel. From coasters of a couple of thousand tons, to gigantic cargo vessels of a hundred thousand tons and more. From Cork to Venezeula, Amsterdam to Capetown, we visited them all. We loaded timber in Scandnavia, grain in Australia, coal in Columbia, ore and minerals from all around the coastline of the African continent. He'd taken crude from the Persian Gulf to gigantic refineries in every country on the globe.

We cursed and praised dockers of every nationality, in every port we visited. We drank and arm-wrestled with those same men at night in dock-side bars from Dublin to Durban, as good-time girls plied their trade in the background. He told me that in apartheid ravaged Africa, it was a crime to consort with the coloureds, as the natives were known. It was punishable by a minimum of nine lashes and immediate deportation.

We drank, then almost as an afterthought, we drank some more. Large creamy-headed pints, slaked a thirst we didn't have, but we drank them anyway.It flowed down our necks as we righted the wrongs of a world that no longer had any real need of us.

We sang songs, or thought we did. Words spilled out without rhyme or reason. Nobody objected. We were past caring. We ran the gauntlet of the top shelf and drank whiskey, large ones and toasted each other. About nine o'clock I soft-shoe-shuffled my way to door, but with the infallible wisdom of a drunk, I veered off course and drifted back to the bar stool. Half an hour later I peered at my new-found friend. He was focussing through one eye. I thought I was stll talking sense, but of course I wasn't. We were well and truly plastered, but no stopping until the bar-room spun out of control. When the counter jumped up and hit me in the forehead for the second time, I got an inkling that maybe it was time to go home. At the street corner we fell against the wall. My new-found friend gave me his parting shot.

'Left home at at sixteen boy,' he said. 'We took the turn of the tide. I steamed down the Lee on my first ship, bound for Rotterdam. When we rounded Roche's Point and the swell lifted her bows, I was proud, proud as a boy could ever hope to be. It was the 8th day of December 1948.' I nearly collapsed.

'What time was the tide?' I asked.

He thought for a moment before giving me an answer that knocked me for six.

I'm Cork city born and I was bawling my way into the world in a nursing home just up from McCurtin Street, at that very time. He'd been hardly a stone's throw from my cradle. I'm a great believer in fate. We were destined to meet. There's no other explanation that will satisfy me.

We parted company. Drifted apart and steamed towards different horizons. I often think of him, that once-met stranger. I never saw him before that day. I never saw him again. I never even learned his name.

Wherever he may be, I'd like him to know that of all the buckles, this was the one I liked best. Someday he said he's teach me to splice rope. Sadly, that day never came.

A Fragment of Time in West Clare

'What did you say ailed you at all?'

The door of the apartment slammed shut behind me. The words, 'Don't come back without one,' were still ringing in my ears as I made my way on to the street. Deserted, but for the presence of man, on the upper reaches of a tall ladder.

'Excuse me,' I said. No reply. I tried again, louder the second time. 'Excuse me, I wonder can you help me?'

The man on the ladder gave no indication that he'd heard, if he had, he must not have thought that my query warranted a reply. He just rested his paint brush across the top of his container of paint and placed the two carefully on the window ledge. Slowly, very slowly he descended to ground level. He stood facing me, looking me up and down for the better part of a minute. At last he condescended to grant me the benefit of a reply.

'Who have I?' He said.

The time was mid-April '97, a warm sunny lunchtime in Kilkee, Co. Clare. Far too early for the summer season, the streets were deserted. The painter on the ladder had been the only person in sight. My problem was a small one. All it needed was someone with a modicum of knowledge to solve it. As is said, *'If in doubt ask.'* Though sometimes there comes a moment when somethings are better left unsaid.

How the situation arose was that I had been employed in Moneypoint Power Station in West Clare on a long-term contract. My partner came with me and we rented an apartment in the centre of Kilkee. We'd brought the television with us. As I'd be working a twelve hour shift, six nights a week for twenty-six weeks, my partner reckoned she'd need something to while away the nights. The best laid plans don't always work out. Hence the problem, the remote control had been forgotten and we couldn't tune the damn thing. It had never once crossed my mind, that television tuning was on a par with rocket science or brain surgery, but as I quickly found out, West Clare was a place quite unlike any other.

'What did you say ailed you at all?' The man on the footpath asked the question, cleared his throat and landed a big globule of spit within an inch of the toe of my boot. Phew! A close one. I moved back a pace.

'I just wondered if you could direct me to a shop where I might get a television remote?' I replied.

He digested the information for what seemed like an hour but was probably a minute. This man was quick on the uptake.

'Television, you say?' He said again.

'That's right, television, I can't tune the damn thing without a remote control.'

'Oh well! You came to the right man, faith then you did.'

My spirits suddenly lifted. 'Oh! That's great! Then you can do it?'

'No! No! No! My dear man, that's not what I said at all. Sure I'd have no truck with the likes of them yokes, but follow me, I know a man who can.'

He walked around the corner, me following and turned into the next street, stopped and pointed. 'Now! See that big blue house up there at the corner?'

I looked in the direction his paint spattered finger was pointing.

'I do.' I replied dutifully. Instructions followed.

'Well that's not the house you're looking for. Go down that street and three doors down you'll come on a house with an open front door. Look in. Inside, you'll see a man eating his dinner at the kitchen table. He's the one you want. Just shout your business in to him and when he's finished eating, he'll put you right. Tell him I sent you. Good-day to you.'

He turned to walk away.

'What did you say your name was?' Says I.

'I didn't, but sure he'll know me anyway.'

Perplexed, I wiped the sweat from my forehead, and decided to carry out the instructions of my departing informant. I turned right at the blue house. One, two, I approached the third door slowly. Sure enough, it was open. a man seated at the table, was tucking into a mountain of spuds and what I took to be bacon and cabbage.

'Hello,' I said. 'Hello.' No answer.

The man paused in mid-stroke, a forkful of bacon, a mere split second from disappearing. He didn't even glance in my direction. 'Yerra would ye stop that shouting, would you? Come in, sit down, I'll be with you when I'm ready.'

Judging by the amount of food, still to be consumed, I reckoned I was in for a long wait. I was wrong. The cutlery rattled and in a matter of minutes the plate was left bare naked. He made to push back his chair, thought better of it, opened the buckle of his trousers and gave a thunderous belch. This was followed seconds later, by the passing of wind, in a barrage of farting so loud, it would have vied with a twenty-one gun salvo of cannon fire.

'Ahh! That's better. Nothing to be gained by keeping it locked up. Now, me decent man, what can I do for you?'

I explained my predicament. Balancing on the two back legs of his chair, he leaned back and hooked his thumbs into the waist-band of his trousers. I assumed he was giving due consideration to my request. How foolish of me. He wasn't even listening.

'How will Cork do in the hurling this year?'

Clueless, I hadn't known they were even playing. Some twenty minutes later, after discussing the weather, the state of the country, the sheep subsidy, how Clare hurlers were the best in the country and the scandalous price of drink, we at last arrived at the matter in hand.

'I was told you were the man to see if I wanted a television tuned.' I said

'Hah! It was your man that sent you up here told you that I suppose?'

'Can you do it?' I asked.

'Can I do it? Under normal circumstances they'd be no better man, the trouble is I'm after giving it up.'

I took a deep breath and counted to fifteen. All the while thinking as rapidly as the swiftly rising panic would allow. Had I heard him right? Since when had television tuning been deemed a vice in West Clare. Had it been passed in a Bill through the Seanad, of which I wasn't aware. The thought process ground to a halt. The first three words I could think of were all the same and all began with a huge capital F.

The Kilkee man had the answer. 'Follow me,' he commanded.

I followed him to the front door. In much the same was as the previous individual he vaguely waved a finger in the direction I should take. 'Go across the town to Ketts bar. At this time of day there will be a man at the bar partaking of a drop of whiskey. He's the man for your job. Don't think for a minute that he'll do as good a job as I would myself, but his skills will be adequate enough for your purpose.'

I made to go. A hand blocked my passage. The Kilkee man was deep in thought. 'No, I'm not thinking straight. Forget about him. He's a good enough man, mind you, the trouble is he has a weakness for the dropeen and whatever might be going with it. No! Give him a wide berth. You'd never be finished paying him. An empty glass would be raised everytime you'd see him and Lord God I've seen it happen, but it's a dear job it could well turn out to be, for with that fellow, a bird never flew on one wing.'

I glanced at my watch. Over an hour had passed. I was no nearer an answer. I was wrong. My new-found adviser had a Plan B.

'This is your best bet. At twenty-to-seven this evening stand out on the footpath outside your front door. It's Mrs. Ryans place you'd be staying isn't it?'

'It is, but how did you know that?'

The Kilkee man ignored my query. 'About that time a red van will be approaching from the direction of Kilrush. Flag it down. Explain your predicament to the driver and tell him I sent you, he'll sort you out. Is that okay with you?'

I just nodded dumbly. To my naive way of thinking what I'd listened to for the previous hour was beyond belief.

'What did you say your name was?' Says I.

'It doesn't matter, he'll know me anyway.'

The door closed behind me. I crawled away, deflated and defeated. Five minutes after, back in the apartment, I found the television working perfectly.

A miracle? No! The forgotten remote control had through some quirk of fate had mysteriously materialised in the bottom of my partners hand-bag. Long moment, deep breath, bite tongue and stay silent. Such is life.

The Colour of Summer

'No shame in crying boy, sometimes it takes a man to do that'

Almost invisible to the human eye the fly flew through the air; the speed was breath-taking. To anyone watching it was just a flash of colour that might have been imagined. To the naked eye it was just something coloured with the hues of the rainbow, visible for a split second before it settled on the water.

The reel hissed and whirred as the line paid out from the tip of the rod. The fly when caught in the pull of the current drifted lazily downstream. The river was shallow here just before it entered a large deep pool. Green river weeds floated on the surface, the small white flowers that grew profusely from the dark mass of its foliage, lay like a tangled necklace on the water. A large chestnut tree on the riverbank shrouded the pool in deep shadow. Here and there like spotlights sunbeams found a gap in the large green leaves and flickered like diamonds on the dark waters of the pool.

A small brown Sand Martin exited its nest high on the riverbank and flew low across the surface of the water. The white on its breast feathers flashed for an instant in the sunlight as it cleared the rim of the pool and climbed skywards.

It was a beautiful evening; the sort of evening a good summer deserves and is remembered for. An almost cloudless Cerulean blue sky stretched as far as the eye could see. Into this haven of blue the few intruding clouds floated high above the landscape like discarded scraps of cotton wool. The first tinges of pink, like candy coloured smudges crested the distant hills as the sun began its long slow descent towards the western horizon.

The trunk of a long dead tree lay where it had fallen. Decaying, its bare branches protruded high above the reed beds; dark and menacing against the blue of the sky like the rib cage of a long extinct dinosaur. Yawning, the old man stretched and settled himself more comfortably against the crumbling bark. Whittling a piece of wood with a pocket-knife he was forming it lovingly into the shape of a boat. It was a good boat. The blade was as sharp as a scalpel and the old man had an eye for detail.

Pushing back the battered hat he wore he paused to blow some errant wood chippings from his creation. Laying the boat on the soft clay of the riverbank he folded the knife, stowing it carefully in a pocket of his faded cotton shirt. With the aid of a stick and not without effort he forced his stiff muscles into motion, hauling himself slowly to his feet. Sweat formed on his brow. Pulling a grubby handkerchief from the pocket of his worn corduroy trousers he dabbed at his forehead. Phew! It gets a little harder every day he thought.

He wouldn't have classed himself as old. Good God no! Others thought differently but what of it? Doctor *Tests and Tablets'* for one, closely followed by his own daughter. Jesus! Was family loyalty a thing of the past? Where was it when needed? With a savage swing of his stick he beheaded a nettle.

He was reasonably fit and could still enjoy a few pints of stout at his leisure. True! Even though he never mentioned to anyone about the tightness he sometimes felt in his chest or the recurring pains in his left arm. On damp days it seemed to be worse, so the answer was obvious. Arthritis! That's all it could be. Why give them one more stick to beat him with? The girl would have wrapped him in cotton wool if she knew so no point in worrying her. They'd have him dead and buried just to prove to themselves how decrepit he really was. No doubt they meant well but what did they know? Nothing! They were hardly peering behind the cracks in the facade.

The girl was the stuff of diamonds, her and the boy. No! He wouldn't wish for changes; it was a fool didn't know when he had it all.

The boy standing knee-deep in water was wielding the fishing rod with the dexterity of a circus ringmaster. Flicking the thick shock of blue-black hair back from his forehead he frowned in determined concentration.

The boy was his daughter's only child. his grandson. Leaning on his stick the old man watched as he cast the fly exactly as he had been shown. He looked at the way he expertly flicked his wrist to land the fly on an imaginary spot on the water. The fierce intensity on the face of the angler filled the eyes of the man with pride.

'Come on lad! Make that the last one for today; your ma will have the supper on the table. We'll not keep her waiting, tomorrow that fish will still be there.'

Looking up, the hair on the boy's forehead flopped across his eyes. The disgruntled tone in his voice was unmistakable.

'Aaw Grandad! There's no rush; any way I'm not hungry. You go on home and tell me ma leave mine in the oven. I'll be alright here.'

The voice of the old man held an edge as he answered. 'No! You can tell her yourself as soon as we get home and hear the answer she'll give you.'

'Ah Grandad! Just another half an hour, ma won't mind. what d'ye say?'

The wheedling tone in the boy's voice almost melted the man's resolve; it took willpower not to surrender to the pleading. Struggling to keep from chuckling he had to turn his head so the boy wouldn't see the smile crinkling the corners of his mouth. Taking off his hat he wiped the sweatband with the tips of his calloused fingers, slowly.

'I'll tell you what I'll say, one more cast and you're done for the day.'

Suddenly, before the boy could respond the tip of the rod jerked and bent in an arc towards the water. The reel screamed as the line paid out almost pulling him off balance. Gripping the rod fiercely with both hands, knuckles white with the effort, he fought to keep his footing. 'Hey Grandad! I've got a bite,' he screamed excitedly.

The old man felt the blood rushing to his head as his heart thumped erratically. 'So you have. Easy now lad, easy; tire him out, you don't want to lose him.'

Ignoring the water pouring over the tops of his stout leather boots and drenching the legs of his trousers he hobbled to the boy's side. He didn't interfere; it was important for the boy to do this on his own. It wasn't every day a ten-year-old got a chance to land what promised to be the catch of a lifetime.

The small deep brown muscles on the boy's arms bulged with effort as the fish ran, taking most of the line. Then as suddenly as it started it stopped.

'Okay lad. Take it easy, reel in some slack, slowly, very slowly. Jesus! Don't rush! Give him time. If he runs again let him go or he'll break the line.'

The fish did run, several times. Turning the reel slowly the boy's fingers trembled. It made one last effort to regain its freedom but its effort lost momentum just before it lost the will to live.

The boy took up the slack on the line and spun the reel until the head of the fish broke the surface of the pool.

'Oh Grandad! It's huge! What a whopper! Jesus! Will ya look at the fuckin' size of him?'

His outburst earned him a barely felt clip on the ear.

'Hey! The lord has enough on his plate without you taking his name in vain. Any more swearing out of you and that fish goes back in the water.'

Shoulders slumping the boy made a half-hearted attempt to sound contrite. 'Sorry Grandad, it just slipped out is all.'

Lying on the surface of the pool, its mouth opening and shutting as it gasped for air, the tail of the fish was twitching slowly. The multi-hued sheen of its scales gleamed like polished silver as it lay in a beam of sunlight on the inky dark water.

'Haul him in now, he's all yours.'

The fish was landed; the silvery blue of its scales dulled as it died.

'You done well boy; he's at least three, maybe three and a half pounds,' the old man estimated. He's probably the biggest ever taken from this pool.'

Excitement gripped the boy causing him to dance from foot to foot; praise from his grandad was something not earned lightly. His chest swelled with pride as he watched his grandfather remove the hook from the mouth and thread a long reed through the gills to use as a carrying handle.

'Here you carry it.' The old man handed the fish to his grandson.

Stooping, he picked up the boat he had been whittling and tossed it as far as he could across the water. They watched, man and boy together as it drifted across the dark surface of the pool before the pull of the current took it and it rushed headlong downriver. In a heartbeat it was lost to sight.

'Come on boy, last one home gets to clean it.'

They had come to some limestone steps that formed a crossing from one field to another; on the top step the boy stopped suddenly. 'Hey Grandad! Look at that.'

Pulling on his grandfather's shirtsleeve as he spoke, the boy was pointing at the setting sun, now sinking like a blood red orb below the skyline of the far-off hills.

'Beautiful isn't it? That's the real colour of summer.'

As if he'd been slapped the old man stopped. 'What did you say?'

Surprised at the sharpness of his grandfather's tone the boy looked up. The smile that moments before had been splitting his chubby features froze on his face.

'The sunset Grandad! It's beautiful! I think that's the real colour of summer.'

The old man looked down, his voice sounded hoarse and cracked slightly with emotion as he spoke. 'Sit awhile lad, don't tire yourself out, that fish is no light load.

The boy sat gratefully on the bottom step, the fish across his lap.

Suspended like a web, the silence hung between them as

the old man lay on the grass. Propping himself up on his elbows, he looked across the fields at his daughter's house. Turf smoke was rising, a lazy white against the blue of the sky. The scent of wildflower's permeated the air. Only sounds of the countryside intruded.

Catching the last of the sun's heat a bumblebee went flitting by their heads to buzz around the blossoms on a bramble bush. Swallows ducked and dived as a sparrow hawk hovering high above them searched the ground for prey. Across the field a farmhand whistled loudly as his dog herded the cows in for evening milking. The sudden tolling of the Angelus bell alarmed a dog fox lurking near the woodland; it barked before creeping deeper into cover.

As if it was a signal he'd been waiting on, slowly and hesitantly the old man began to speak. 'There are things you should know, and I think it's time you should be knowing them.'

Glancing at the boy, he satisfied himself he had his attention. 'What I tell you now is not something I often speak of so bear with me.'

Nodding, the boy listened. The old man didn't suffer fools gladly or waste words, if he'd something to say it would be important.

'I was born and raised in that cottage where your ma is living now. It's funny how I can remember that time as if it was yesterday, but I can't think what I had for breakfast this morning. No blue-sky day then, thunder was in the air and the sky was a deep dark magenta, an ominous sort of colour. That was the day the girl came to stay.'

She'd come from London to spend the school holidays with her grandmother, our nearest neighbour. My mother took me up to make her welcome. She actually had to drag me kicking and screaming every yard of the way. I nearly wore the toes from my boots trying to delay the inevitable. Oh Lord! You should have seen me.'

The old man chuckled at the memory.

'I couldn't see any reason to greet visitors and a girl at that. How quickly I changed my mind. The first time I saw her she was standing beneath an old dog rose in her grand-mother's garden. The small pink buds were framing her head like a halo against the backdrop of that deep purple sky; I thought nobody could ever look so beautiful. From that moment on I was captivated. She had an odd name that I could never quite get my tongue around; it was years later before I found out that it meant summer.'

'Back there in that pool we fished for tawnies with a net and jar and paddled in the river. We caught bees in old jam-pots and I showed her where the white-owl roosted in the hayloft. We fed chickens and searched for eggs; all the things of importance that children of that age find to do. She'd gather honeysuckle, woodbine, and fuchsia from the hedgerows, but ox-eye daisies and buttercups were her favourites. She could sit for hours making garlands of wild-flowers, and weaving daisy chains. Every day we grew a little closer.'

Though she came back year after year for the holidays that first time was a summer coloured by magic. The sort of summer that when it ends you know you'll never see the likes of it again.'

The old man took off his hat; scratching his head he twirled the hat slowly between his fingers before continuing.

'She went back to London and I sobbed my heart out

for every minute of about a day and a half. That's what you do at your age, you get a setback and you think the world is about to end. It doesn't, believe me it just feels that way.'

Replacing the hat on his head he picked a blade of grass, chewing idly on it for a few moments before speaking again.

'At Christmas I got a card and a promise to return the following year; the promise was kept. After the old lady, her granny, passed away the visits stopped. We still kept in touch; long letters about twice a year and a card for my birthday and Christmas.'

Were they tears he saw in the old man's eyes? Hardly! A man as tough as that wouldn't cry over a girl, would he?

'Did you ever see her again Grandad?' The boy asked.

The old man continued his narrative, seeming not to hear the question. 'I was turned twenty when I first left this place. Work was scarce, jobs impossible to find. I remember being taken out of school to pick potatoes, anything that might put a bit extra on the table. It was just the way of things. Those with jobs in banking or the professions, had to be the sons or daughters of business people, the wealthy and such. The child of a labouring man had no chance.

Girls were thought fit for little else but rearing babies and doing housework. Boys were just brought up to take the boat. To this day every family in these parts has someone in America. The harsh reality was a never-ending circle; once they left, there was no coming back.

'When I went myself it wasn't for adventure, but necessity. It was a case of work or starve. I had no idea England was so big. I can still remember the signs in pub windows and eating houses, *No Dogs or Irish'* No one hung out a shingle to welcome me. I didn't know of anyplace else, so I went to London.

'She invited me to stay with her mother and herself in their flat in Camden Town. I slept on their sofa for a month or more and was glad of it. I couldn't count the times I wanted to come home, but it wasn't an option. What would I be coming home to? Nothing.

In a way fortune favoured me. The London-Yorkshire highway, what they called the Great North Road was starting. Ah lad! Those were the days; anyone who wanted work got it.

We kept in contact for a few months but then the letters stopped. I wrote a few more times but never got a reply. We were young; I thought maybe she'd forgotten me and moved on with her life.

I was in digs in some backwater of Yorkshire when her mother contacted me. Bad news? Is there any other kind? The love of my life had died unexpectedly. No explanation. They'd got her to hospital and saved the baby, but not her.

Baby? That was the first I knew of it. Real dread has a cold feeling; it was like an ice-cold hand squeezing the life-blood from my veins. Life is sometimes a hard road; it can throw obstacles before you that seem high as mountains. I think that was the day I grew up.

The baby was a girl, hair as black as a crow's wing, she had big brown eyes, just like you. A little sweetheart. When I saw her, love stole my heart for the second time. That's my daughter and your mother, I'm talking about. A few years later when I brought her back here, I realised for the first time that the colour of *Summer* was black.'

My mother raised her. Not without opposition. Ireland

that time was a different place. Hidebound by religion, something like a baby, and a coloured child to boot would have been a scandalous event in a small community.

They came. The pious and the holier than thou brigade. They tried to take the child.

My mother might have been a small slip of a woman, but I'll tell you boy, she had the heart of a lion. She stood out there in our yard and defied the lot of 'em. Priests and do-gooders, she gave them all short shrift. They came back time and again, but she wasn't for giving up her grand-daughter. It wouldn't have been her way. They ostracised her for years, but she weathered the storm.

Nodding his head slowly the boy looked up, understanding in his eyes.

The old man took him in his arms hugging him; feeling the tuck in his heart as the boy struggled to control his sobs. Tears soaked the front of the old man's shirt.

'No shame in crying boy, sometimes it takes a man to do that.'

Ruffling his fingers through the boy's hair, he said. 'Let's go home go home lad. Your ma will be waiting. Have we a pan big enough for that fish?'

Do Seabirds ever Cry this far from Shore?

Fog! I've never seen the like

The water lapping against the sides of the boat is no longer disturbing me. How long has it been since it intruded on my thoughts? Who could tell? More than hours certainly, probably days, I'd remember if it was a week, wouldn't I?

Why is everything so white? Has colour ceased to exist? No! The bright red heavy wool coat I'm wearing still shows a semblance of colour through the thick layers of hoarfrost that's clinging to its ridges and folds. Quality is not easy to hide.

I had stolen the coat, but I do not consider myself a thief. A thief might have sold it on for a trifle of its value, but I had taken it out of necessity. It's my shame to live with or most likely die with it, but a thief? No! I was brought up better than that.

A scream shatters the frozen silence. The sound of a disembodied voice echo's across the water, before dissipating into sobs.

Fog! I've never seen the likes; thick and white it is, thicker even than a good wool blanket. It's covering everything. I can feel it now sticking like burrs in the back of my throat, creeping deeper by the minute, freezing the tissue of my lungs. Christ! It's so hard to breathe, just how much colder can it get?

Earlier a man seated nearby was cursing loudly when his whole body was shaken by a paroxysm of coughing and choking, at first I thought he might be throwing a fit and I stretched forward to help, but he cleared his throat and spat a wad of thick green phlegm over the side. I thanked God there was no wind.

There's not so many in this boat. I have a seat to myself but that doesn't mean I think I'm lucky. My sister Elly, God love her, should sitting right here beside me; that would be lucky.

Fresh tears are stinging my eyelids and as I think of her. Arm in arm we were promenading on a deck high above the ocean when the siren sounded. It blew and blew; loud it was, the sound mournful.

Being steerage passengers, we shouldn't have been on the deck; we'd been warned about the consequences of an infringement of that rule but then aren't regulations always made to be broken?

'... if any of you Paddys are caught parading around the decks it'll more than my bloody job's worth. I don't make the rules; I just have to enforce 'em. If ye play ball with me and don't make life difficult I just might turn a blind eye so a few of ye can take a stroll around the top deck. All I'm asking is ye don't get caught, just make sure it's dark; very dark.'

As God is my judge, an Englishman he might have been, but he was of the people, and had stamp of decency about him. I never saw him again.

I don't remember much. Jesus! How the hell did we even get in the water?

'Iceberg!' Someone shouted, then everyone was shouting the same thing. I had no idea what an iceberg was, never having seen one; I did not have long to wait.

Chaos is not a word that would adequately describe what

happened in the mayhem that followed amidst the confusion of shadows and screams.

I felt a thump; seconds later a shudder ran through the timbers of the deck and the ship stopped moving. An unearthly shriek like the wailing of a banshee drowned out all other sounds; it only lasted a moment before the ship continued on course.

Whatever had happened was not of our doing. We were at the head of the companionway leading down to the steerage when the nightmare began. Before we could take another step, the world had fallen into hell.

Just above our heads an anonymous voice boomed. *'ABANDON SHIP!'* As if they'd come from nowhere people were running blindly in all directions. I had no idea that panic could spread so rapidly; like wildfire, quicker than I could blink.

Men with the fear of God in their eyes were hustling woman and children along the decks. The voice kept booming. 'Abandon ship!'

'Ah sure that can't be right,' someone shouted. 'Didn't they say she was unsinkable?'

We should have been fortunate; we were next to a boat but luck rewards those born lucky. A man was bellowing orders as we moved forwards.

'Women and children! Don't panic! Women and children to the front, plenty of room for all but ...'

A burly man wearing a stovepipe hat burst to the front of the waiting throng. 'There's not enough boats! I paid good money so don't tell me I can't get a seat.'

Spitting with fury he roared a tirade of abuse into the face of the boatman. The ship lurched, ropes snapped and the lifeboat half-filled with screaming women and children vanished from sight. The abusive man snatched at a rope, missed, and careened screaming into the darkness.

The boatman was looking right at me as he shrugged his shoulders. It might have been a trick of the flickering lights, but I saw despair in his eyes, I know I did.

Somewhere in the darkness a bow lovingly caressed the strings of a violin. An orchestra played a final serenade.

It was no trick of the light or shadow play; this was real. I could only gape.

Mother of God! Did anyone ever see anything so beautiful? As the moonlight danced off its facet's I thought at first it might have been an apparition. Brighter than the finest of diamonds, its whiteness dazzled. Blues! As I've only ever imagined them to be. From the translucence of near whiteness to the dark mysterious blues of the depths on which it floated, this majestic vision had them all.

Magnificent! It truly was. Foaming white-capped waves prostrated themselves around its base as if in homage to greatness far beyond my understanding.

The deck tilted suddenly. Just as suddenly people were running uphill, not going anywhere, but running as if the devil was snapping at their heels.

Jostled, I lost my footing then just as suddenly we were tumbling downhill. Over and over we went; rag dolls at the mercy of providence; then we were falling, falling... It seemed as if forever.

Elly! At seventeen, two years younger than me; now destined to stay that age forever. One minute she was clutching my arm, both of us struggling as we clambered for a place in the boat; then she was gone. I could only watch unbelievingly as time stood still. Gone! My last sight was of the silent scream etched for eternity on her thin features before the water closed above her head as she sank beneath me.

Gone! The apple of my father's eye; some protector I turned out to be. Someone wrenched my arm and I landed in an undignified bundle in the bottom of the boat.

I'm on my own now with no idea of where I am, but in that respect I'm no worse off than anyone else. Everything has gone! All I've left to my name are the clothes that I'm wearing, not much to show for nineteen years of hardship.

Isn't it strange, how in the space of a heartbeat, the course of a person's existence can change forever? Would my dreams of the New World and the better life I'd hoped for, ever come to fruition?

A sliver of ice has fallen from my hair. From the seat opposite an elderly man is staring at me. A needle of ice that would not be out of place in a sewing box, is dangling from the end of his nose. His frost-coated eyebrows remind me of a winter hedgerow stretching across a forehead with more furrows than a ploughed field.

I'm wrong! The man isn't staring at me. His eyes are bereft of reason; he's staring at nothing, nothing at all.

My name is Margaret Olden and I came here from the lower harbour of Cork. Born in 1893, I'm fourth eldest from a family of twelve, five boys and seven girls. When my brothers reached sixteen, they crossed to Great Island, and from there to God knows where; I never saw them again. When I say we had nothing, nothing was what we had, not a shoe to fit our feet. Piss poor we were. Even worse we didn't have a pot to piss in.

Born as slaves to time and tide, from the youngest to

the oldest, we scrimped an existence from what could be gleaned along the shoreline. Seasonal work; picking shellfish, chopping seaweed, picking potatoes; scavenging if we had to, if it needed doing it was what we did. It's called surviving. Now and again, being the oldest I got some work in the big house with my mother. That's where my fine red coat came from.

The lady of the house wore this coat to the service in East Ferry church on Christmas mornings; elegance itself she looked. It's the only thing I ever envied, and I was taken by it long before I took it. The coat wouldn't be missed for eight months and anything could happen in that time. I suppose it was the devil stoking the foolish fire of pride in me, but I wanted to arrive in New York like I'd come from better things. My mother would have whipped the skin from my backside for my vanity.

When my eldest brother Willie sent the fare for two of us to join him; it was decided that Elly and myself would be the ones to go. As surely as Spring tides flooded our road, I knew that coat would be going with me.

A man in the front of the boat is hallooing through cupped hands. It seems not to matter that his voice is failing to pierce the icy vapour and he is completely undeterred that his calls go unanswered. Wearing a long dark overcoat that might be blue or black with some sort of gold twine stitched around the cuffs, the man has the bearing of an officer. The peak of his cap is braided with the same twine.

The silence is almost eerie, how quiet it is, just the lapping of water against the creaking timbers of the boat. Now and again the swish of a waterlogged rope and the voice that will be ingrained on my memory to my dying day...

'HALLOO, HALLOO.'

Shifting my position, I notice again the fierce intensity of the cold that prevents any heat from invading my body. Cold! Lifeless and clammy as a corpse, it's wrapped itself around my soul. It's what I imagined might be the cold of a tomb.

There are no raised voices. Would it always be this way? Do seabirds ever cry this far from shore? It's daylight; somewhere above the fog the sun must be shining. Would I ever again marvel at the simple magic of sunbeams waltzing on water?

A lonely heart makes a heavy load, my grandmother often told me. The truth of her words were brought home to me, that morning we took Mick Galligan's boat from the East Ferry pier to Great Island and walked the road to Queenstown.

There was no laughter amongst the crowds thronging the White Star Line jetty, but sobs were frequent. On every corner last minute embraces, tearful goodbyes and promises to write were repeated over again.

Huge! Aptly named Titanic, for a titan it was. The black bulk of the ship blotted out the skyline as it rode at anchor on the Whitegate Roads. The cathedral bells were tolling from the hill above Queenstown as we climbed the ladder to the deck high above us.

Elly crossed herself. 'God love'em,' she said. 'It must be somebody's funeral.'

Why is it so silent? Surely someone's voice should be raised in a prayer or hymn to give thanks for our survival, but there is nothing, nothing, nothing...

Luck is a Four-letter Word

Some days it was good, there were days it could be better

Jimmy 'No Mates' Murphy belched loudly and pushed his plate away. The dinner as usual had been eaten in silence. A knife fell to the floor, but as was his want, he ignored it. Picking it up would never have crossed his mind, that useless article he was tied to would only go getting the wrong impression.

Wearing a smile full of malice, he staggered from the table. She'd only go thinking something stupid; like that he still loved her. Bloody woman! Stupid was too kind a word for her.

His long-suffering wife stared after his departing back. Distaste etched itself on her tired features as she took in the loathsome sight. His trouser crotch at knee level gave the impression of a flag hanging limply at half-mast. Defying gravity, how it managed to stay up was well beyond the laws of physics.

He was leaving her. He hadn't said anything; he didn't need to. Something like that took courage, but she could read the signs. Changing his underwear without reminding, the bathroom constantly stinking of cheap lotions and whatever that God-awful stuff he was using to keep that stupid comb-over in place. He'd even taken to washing his teeth.

Sipping slowly at a tumbler of water she toyed with her half-eaten meal. What use was it all? She'd asked herself

– 133 –

that question more times every day than there were beads on a rosary. Back in the day when she still believed a priest had told her that God moved in mysterious ways. They certainly mystified her. With eyes raised heavenwards she pleaded for the one piece of luck that would change her life forever.

The toilet flushed two minutes before his footsteps pounded down the stairs and the front door slammed. If he didn't come home would she miss him? If she never saw him again would she care? No! The answer was a definite no on both counts.

That night God again saw fit to move mysteriously; Jimmy 'No Mates' didn't come home.

Annie-May Murphy's little shop yielded her an income of sorts. Some days it was good, some days it might have been better. She dealt in everything; bric-a-brac of all sorts but her life-long love was old paintings. To learn more about those people, who with brushes and colour could give life to their dreams was her burning passion.

For hours the man had been shuffling about the shop, watching her. She was about to close when he approached and proffered his card. Yes! He represented the one of the big auction houses. The painting? Without doubt a Vermeer. Value? Hmm! Something is only worth what a collector would pay. Certainly millions, but the sky was the limit. Her life changing moment had arrived.

'You have provenance. Will you sell?' He asked.

She replied. 'It's what I'm here for, make me an offer.'

Somewhere beside the Cork-Midleton rail-line the body of a middle-aged male was lying between a rock and a hard place. Crows screamed raucously.

Stretching and yawning, God rolled the dice again, another six. Twice in a row. She was on a roll. Pausing, she rubbed her chin, one more before dinner? Who should it be? Caucasian, black, male or female? Did it really matter? She closed her eyes and rolled the dice again. Scratching out a name, she turned to the next page.

The Silly Girl

'You're the fairest one of all...'

The silly girl shook out the long blonde tresses of her hair. She felt a bit giddy and light-headed from the wine she'd had earlier, but so what? That's the way one was supposed to feel at parties. After all this was Dublin; it was the zenith of the Celtic Tiger era and what else could one do only party like there was no tomorrow.

She breathed deeply, admiring for the hundred time that evening her reflection in yet another mirror. The heavily made up image gazing back at her seemed to say, 'You've got it all girl, and you're the fairest one of all.'

God, she felt so good; this was what living was all about. Sure, some people had died from what she was about to do, quite a few in fact, but they were just no-brainers, people of no consequence. Nobody even missed people like that. Such a fate would never befall someone on the top rung of the ladder like she was. Dying was strictly for the nobodies.

Stooping over the little table she sniffed the line of snow-white powder through a rolled-up bank note. This displayed affluence; a century note showed style, a five 'C' note was real class and she reckoned she had class in spades.

She sniffed deeply, this was just so cool, surely things couldn't ever get much better than this. What a buzz!

Days later the feeling is much cooler. Though she doesn't know it the temperature has dropped right off the scale. The only buzz now is from the saw the pathologist is holding and the mortuary table is at that moment part of the coolest game in town. Much cooler than vodka laced with ice. Though not so cold as the features of her parents frozen in grief, captured for all time in a hospital waiting room by the fluorescent glare of media flashlights.

The silly girl craved the attention of those lights; with a relentless hunger for fame, she stopped at nothing to grab headlines. No stunt was too demeaning or bizarre. She existed only for life before the lens. Revelling in the glare of the spotlights, she was born to seen. She thought she had it all. A life in the fast lane and (unfortunately for her) an all too brief moment of fame. The silly girl had all the answers, but she couldn't handle the moment.

In stony fields on the mountains of Afghanistan the white poppies will bloom again. Deep in the jungles of Columbia undernourished, impoverished peasants will collect a pittance for their harvest, barely enough to stay alive. They never know the true value of their crops or have any idea of the destruction indirectly wrought by their labour.

White and stiff the silly girl will now never reach maturity, decaying before ever bearing fruit. It was far too high a price to pay for a mention in a few columns of newsprint and a glimpse at that ever-elusive moment of fame.

She had friends, night owls, attracted to the limelight like moths to a flickering candle. Funny now how the light no longer fascinates. Darkness suddenly is a newfound friend. Now more than anything they crave anonymity. he blackness of night and the darkest shadows of alleyways welcome them to its bosom, hugging them close. When she needed them most, they ran faster than diarrhoea, those good friends, vanishing quicker then spots treated with Clearasil.

On Social Media outlets sympathies for her abound, it would appear she was everybody's friend. The heavily made up faces of would be celebrities, mascara running with tears, fill the screens.

On Christmas morning carols will be sung in churches across Dublin. "The Season to be Jolly" will jingle from bells north and south of the Liffey, no doubt bonhomie will abound. When the foggy dew finally lifts, the Christmas present the parents of the silly girl will most remember is their daughter's body, forever gift-wrapped in an undertaker's shroud.

A year or so from now a new generation of wannabes will say 'Who? I don't really remember. Oh her! Ah yes, of course I do. She overdosed. Wasn't she a silly girl?'

Death with a Capital 'D'

She cried, then cried again...

Ellie Riordan hadn't wanted to die, but than which of you does? Have you ever wondered why, at the last gasp of breath, the dying one always struggles to prolong life? It's why the hanged man always dances at the end of the rope, he mightn't want to do it, but choice is not an option; he has to dance with death. Strauss never wrote music to suit the last steps of the condemned; he never wrote a Last Waltz for an execution reprieve.

Have any of you ever seen death, violent death in close-up? I'm not talking about the celluloid imagery of the silver screen. You can walk away from that. Outside the cinema doors after a few nervous giggles, that type of death pales into insignificance. Five minutes later, munching on a burger, it's history. It's not real and subconsciously you know that make-belief death can't break through your comfort zone. It can't throttle the life from you and scare you shit-less. Real death can. Death that comes when least expected. Suddenly and violently.

Death as it came to Ellie Riordan, that's a death will make you realise that adrenaline flows in various shades of brown.

Violent death is never pleasant, and in the aftermath usually leaves a silence so quiet you can cut it. No pain, that's long gone; just a silence that chokes the life out of all other sounds. Oh yes, I nearly forgot to mention, the whole scene is usually painted with a technicolour visage of blood.

Blood that congeals on floorboards, soaks through cushions and splashes walls and ceilings. That's what blood does. A cut-throat can paint a room quicker than you can blink. Paint it with warm vibrant reds, mixed with splashes of scarlets and crimson worthy of Picasso.

You don't believe me, do you? You think I lie? What fools you are. Who would verify my words? Whom would you ask?

Ask Ellie Riordan, she's been there and who would know better? Go on, she won't bite, she's long passed that; yo u only have to ask, after all she died to tell you. She'll tell you why the cemeteries are full of mouldering corpses, stinking, rotting, putrefying corpses who if life were left to them, would all wish they were elsewhere, just as Ellie Riordan would.

Funny thing about corpse, no matter how much you loved it as a living being, once life is gone it's just a smelly heap of bones and offal, but you know that. That's why people, civilised people like you, bury their dead in cemeteries. They hide them away in holes beneath the ground. Clay, be it black, yellow or brown covers everything. The successes and the failures. What they once loved so much that now they can't bear to look at, waits for judgement day; proving that love doesn't conquer all. Fools, they can't grasp that judgement, for those people has long passed. Don't defend the inexcusable; surely you don't want to stay here just to prolong your pitiful existence? I don't believe that for one moment. Who in their right senses would want to live in this place?

I once overheard a man say, that if he saw death coming, he'd run towards it. I doubt that very much. Why should a perfectly normal, healthy individual say something like that? Think on it, ask yourself the question; does anyone want to die that badly? Ellie Riordan didn't; she didn't want to die at all.

It wasn't that she had many more years left, or that it mattered much if she lived or died; very few would miss her and far less would care.

A quiet woman, *'too quiet for her own good'*, her old mother used always say, and that wasn't today or yesterday.

She was or had been what was once known in the vernacular of the city as a *'sepra'*; a once married woman whose husband had departed. Upped and left. The husband of Ellie Riordan had done just that. He had, like numerous others taken the King's shilling, sworn the oath of allegiance and went off to fight in somebody else's war. He left without even a note to say goodbye. More often out of work than in, and with a lip on him for liquor. He hadn't been a good husband, that would have been too much to hope for She was well shut of him. Some said he did her a favour; at least he never laid a fist on her again.

But back in those days she'd been young. Young and in love. A girl wearing her heart for all the world to see won't believe for an instant that she'd be better off without the man she married. Don't try telling her; you'll not like the answer.

Ellie Riordan, with a child at her breast would have been like that. She would have put a brave face on being condemned to a life alone, and her years still falling short of a full score.

That was back in what they call the dim and distant past. It might have been soon forgotten by most women, but she didn't forget, and for her there was nothing dim about it. The memory was as bright as day.

The child didn't last long. When it died, a part of Ellie Riordan died also. No one was too sure if it was male or female, no one cared. Some said it was a blessing from God.

She had buried it. On Halloween night she had crossed the North Gate bridge and walked across the city with the still warm body of her infant clutched beneath her coat. The river had been flowing swiftly beneath the bridge; she'd paused, dismissed her thoughts and continued walking. It had snowed, but she had walked until she found a freshly covered grave in a Southside cemetery. She had scratched and dug with her bare hands until her skin was raw, and her blood ran free. The blood from her fingers dyed the white of the christening robe. Ellie Riordan laid her child in someone else's grave and said goodbye to love. She didn't just bury an infant; she buried her dreams. Nobody cared.

The world passed her door and life was lonely. In all her years she had never received a birthday card and but for the tinsel in the windows and the crib in the church, she wouldn't think of Christmas. There were good days; those were days that she didn't cry quite as much as she did on bad days, but every day she cried. The unkind tongues said that she was much like her life, simple. It was just the way she chose, she would never be happy, but she had a contentment of sorts.

She worked while she was able at any menial job she got to do; a bit of this, a bit of that, a little of the other, a recipe of toil to keep the wolf from the door. When she could work no more, she had her pension. It wasn't much, but then she was used to very little.

Every morning without fail, whatever the weather, she locked her front door and shuffled down the hill and along the quay to St. Mary's. Hugging the inside of the path, she kept her eyes fixed firmly on the pavement. On her feet the worn soles of somebody else's shoes made no sound amidst the clicking clacking of the shop girl's high heels. If any saw her, they never remembered. She was anonymous.

Last Thursday was just like a lifetime of Thursdays, another day in a routine that never varied; that was the day she picked her way slowly across the bridge. She joined the queue in the post office and drew her pension. The clerk behind the counter couldn't say what she looked like; it wasn't her job to remember people. The records showed she'd drawn her money, so she must have done.

She went in the shopping centre, drifting aimlessly between the aisles. Sometimes she went by the children's section, not to browse, just to remember what life once had to offer. It was that time of year again; later the children would be on the street trick-or-treating. She bought some nuts, a small bag of apples, half-a-dozen lollipops and a small, scented candle for her window; it was Halloween.

The girl on the checkout was cheerful; smiled at her, made a remark about the weather and told her to have a nice day. She had an accent that was foreign, but it was nice not to be ignored, she'd remember to say a prayer for her.

The church of St. Mary's was quiet last Thursday. Across the road and old man leaned on the quay wall where the limestone steps lead down to the river and idly counted the seagulls. A beggar on the steps sat against a pillar and held up an empty cardboard coffee cup as she approached. He smiled, opening a cavern of broken and rotting teeth. She opened her purse.

In the dimness of the church she prayed, cried and prayed again. She lit a candle and left a small offering in a box by the door. It was Thursday, just like any other. When she came out of the church the steps were deserted; the beggar had gone.

The children had come, as she knew they would, laughing and jostling as they argued over the treats. It was children having fun in the way that children do. She liked them to call; they were the only ones that ever did.

She'd been asleep. Something had woken her. It wasn't children, not a child's knock, there it was again, a sort of *'won't take no for an answer'* knock; someone persistent. She forced her old bones out of the armchair and peeped through a chink in the curtains. It was dark outside, and she didn't like the dark. She never went out at night, especially not on Halloween. Louder this time, three angry knocks. Slowly she shuffled across the hall and fearfully opened the door.

She didn't know the man at least not by name, but he looked like someone she should know. She'd seen him somewhere, now where was it?

The first blow broke her nose; the second burst the retina in her right eye. There were a lot more blows and a multitude of kicks; she felt none of them, after the second she was unconscious. Reduced in seconds to an untidy bundle of still breathing second-hand clothes she lay in the hallway of what had been her home, for more than half a century.

He got what he came for, the remains of her pension. He ransacked the house, smashed her few mementos and destroyed what was left of her life.

He didn't find what he really wanted, the loose brick by the fireplace, the hiding place where she kept her savings.

She opened one eye, trying to focus through the blood and pain.

A child stood in the corner, a young child; what was he doing here? She stretched out a hand, trying with the last of her strength to crawl, moaning with the pain of broken ribs and a punctured lung. She had to reach the child; the light was so bright, so wonderfully bright, the light would make her safe.

She never felt the knife that sliced into her throat and opened her from ear to ear; never felt the heaving, panting body that defiled her as she gurgled her life out on the cold linoleum. Ellie Riordan died as she had lived, lonely and afraid, with hope just inches from her fingertips.

Her death had no nobility; it did not come like a tall rider sitting astride a pale horse. Her death came in a '97 white Toyota Starlet, with a noisy exhaust.

That was last Thursday, teatime; this is Tuesday night. Did any of you miss her? If you had the chance now would you call in on her, bring some biscuits and share a pot of tea? Share a few moments of her life, she would have liked that, someone to alleviate her loneliness.

It's too late now, too late by five days and a lot of years. If your bus was five minutes late, you'd moan about it. Five days later and she's still lying on that floor; that's how long since you would last have seen her, that's how long she's been dead.

You people sicken me. To your shame not one of you missed her and none of you cared. What would it have cost you to stop by and say hello? It might have made a difference. Talk is cheap, but words are priceless; they don't cost a damn.

I watched from a distance, as the lowlife that had so casually ended her life, forgot she ever existed. He boozed away her pension in a haze of alcohol fumes and cigarette smoke. He really pissed me off.

He never noticed me watching as the small phial of white powder changed hands in the toilet. He never wondered why his hand shook so much as he mixed the cocktail of drugs and drew far more into the ampoule then intended. He never heard me laughing as he pressed home the syringe. Never wondered why his eyes bulged like a deep-water fish as he swallowed his tongue and a rush with the speed of an express train hit him, as the drugs entered his veins.

Three hours after invading my territory and stepping on my toes, the useless piece of filth died, as he deserved to, on the toilet floor. It was I who judged him, and I made sure he died a painful death. It was the least I could do.

I had liked Ellie Riordan; she was one of life's good souls, she wasn't ready to die, and a death like hers needed avenging. Tomorrow, no one will beg on the steps of St. Mary's.

Who am I? Sometimes I wonder myself. It should suffice to say that I usually call when least expected; but keep an eye out for me. Someday I just might come calling on you. My name? Oh sorry, didn't I mention it? Some people have been known to call me the Grim Reaper. It's Death. I spell it with a capital D.

No Turning Back

He washed his meal down with a small bottle of stout

J acob McCarthy sat down heavily on the old wooden park bench. Like himself, the bench would soon have to be replaced.

The years seemed to slip by faster now and all too soon retirement would be upon him. He sat here every day to eat his lunch and study the racing page of one of the tabloids. He liked it here under the shade of the elms. 'Maybe when I'm gone,' he thought, 'they might dedicate the seat to me'. A little brass plaque with his name on it, just to show he left a mark on the world. The thought amused him, 'fat chance of that happening, that kind of honour was reserved for people who would probably never know that this park existed'.

His lunch never varied but then he was a man of simple tastes. Anything more exotic then the two slices of brown bread, the piece of red cheddar cheese and a slice of ham would have been alien to his nature. He liked to cover the meat and cheese with a layer of brown pickle, the sort with lots of onion in it. He washed his main meal down with a small bottle of stout; and as an added treat on Fridays his landlady always included a small slice of homemade apple pie. For his mid-morning break, he always had a hard-boiled egg with a slice of bread and a cup of tea. The tea was always black, as he had never taken to the stupid idea of milk being processed and interfered with once it left the cow. He liked brown eggs best; he didn't know why his mother had once told him that, but it had stuck in his mind ever since.

'That was a long time ago, must be the bones of fifty years or more,' he mused, though It felt like a lifetime ago.

He'd been in the same digs now through all four seasons of every year for twenty-two years come next January; there had never been a good enough reason to change, it suited him and he was happy with his lot. He liked his landlady, liked the way she called him 'my Mr. McCarthy' when she had reason to mention him to anyone. He thought they had a good relationship; she was good to him, but then maybe he in own way was good to her. It wasn't a boarding house as such and he'd only stumbled across it by accident, but that was obviously meant to be. Wasn't that what was meant by fate?

He wasn't long in London at the time. A big, green as grass young fellow just feeling his way and trying to learn by his mistakes and 'by Christ', he thought, *'back then the mistakes were plenty.'*

He was working on tunnels then for the new Victoria line and he'd been told of digs available up this way. He'd knocked on the door of the wrong house. He apologised to the lady who answered when he realised his mistake and was just going out the front gate when she called him back. She had a spare room he could have.

'How much would it be?' He asked.

She didn't know, so he told her the going rate for bed and breakfast with a bit extra on top for an evening meal if it was provided. She was more than happy with that and showed him the room. He moved in the following day. Over the course of time the rate was adjusted now and then, always at his instigation, and to the mutual satisfaction of both parties. It was an arrangement that worked well for both of them.

He was a tidy person; kept his room in good order and always paid the rent on the day it was due. She had been divorced twice she told him and wouldn't marry again for diamonds. She couldn't hide her surprise when he told he'd never had a steady girlfriend. The dance halls in north London were booming at the time and she encouraged him to go every Saturday night. The weekend haunts of the Irish migrants, the Crown in Cricklewood, the Shamrock in Camden Town. He only went under duress, but eventually he had to tell her that they weren't places he liked to frequent. If you were a hard drinker with no thought of tomorrow, they probably served a need, but he'd seen enough lives ruined by drink to go down that road. Eventually, and in only the way woman can, she wheedled it out him that he was still a virgin.

He didn't know how it came about. He was helping her in the garden one Saturday evening, and the heat was intense. When it got so hot that he had to take his shirt off, she complimented him on his fine physique. God that woman could talk when she'd a mind to. One thing led to another, in the end to shut her up more than anything else; he'd confessed that he knew nothing about women, had never been with a woman and wouldn't know what to do with a woman if he had one. From the corner of his eye he saw the look of total surprise on her face. After a half hour of total silence, he thought he'd fixed her and that would be the end of the matter. Jacob McCarthy was an innocent abroad; he really did know nothing about women.

To be fair to her she didn't force the issue, but on Monday he noticed she'd been to the hairdressers. She'd got it cut and styled and even had a bit of colour put in. He told her it suited her and took years off her. He could see the colour rising in her cheeks.

'I bet you say that to all the girls.' she said, but he could see she was well pleased. On the following Monday she went to the shops. She had gotten her housework done early and had taken a tube down to Oxford St. She'd window shopped for two hours before finally settling on Miss Selfridges and Top Shop, having decided Chelsea Girl was more than a few years too young for her. She'd bought herself a nice top that clung to all the right places and deliberated for a long time over the purchase of new trousers.

'Does my bum look big in this?'

'No!' The assistant had diplomatically assured Madame that they made the very best of her assets. Over the dinner that night he again complimented her on how well she looked.

'Oh it's nothing,' she said. 'Just a few old things I had lying around at the back of the wardrobe for ages. I thought I'd better get a wear out of them before they go out of fashion, styles change so fast these days.

'Ah now,' he said. 'Don't be doing yourself down. You'd have no bother there, a fine woman like you. Even if you were reduced to wearing meal sacks sure you'd still turn heads around here. Aren't you head and shoulders above any woman in this place?'

She blushed a deep crimson. 'Mr.McCarthy, she said, 'You say the nicest things, you really know how to pay a girl a compliment.'

That night she knocked on his door and invited him to join her for a nightcap in the sitting room. On Wednesday night she had invited him to watch a re-run of *Gone with the Wind,* and she'd opened a bottle of wine.

Thinking back now he wasn't sure how the seduction had begun, it must have been the wine, he only knew it had happened and he was glad it had. Before he knew where he was, she had him in her bed. She had been a good teacher; making allowances for his lack of experience and finesse. She'd been understanding and passionate; not rushing him yet taking him so high that at times he thought he'd taken leave of his body, as well as his senses. Thursday had been the first time he had missed a day's work for years.

They'd become lovers after that first night. Nothing written in stone, just two people with a deep respect and understanding of each other's needs. It wasn't a constantly holding hands, till death do us part type of romance; it was deeper than that. Nobody knew of their situation; nobody needed to. The important thing was, that they were there for each other always. They hadn't felt the need to live in each other's pockets to prove that to anyone else, but she did take to calling him Jake, which he rather liked.

He took a mouthful of the frothy brown porter; savouring the taste in his throat before he licked the crumbs of the apple pie off the tips of his fingers. Drink never bothered him much.

She accompanied him to the pub every Sunday at lunchtime; he'd have three or four pints before the dinner, and she'd have two small white wines. Then home for the Sunday roast, a read of the paper and if the day was fine they'd spend the evening pottering about in the garden. He enjoyed watching her as she tended the plants, from the opening of the buds in the springtime to the deadheading of the roses in the autumn. She had a way with plants, and he'd learned a lot from her. It stood him in good stead when he felt unable to work in tunnels anymore and moved to the Municipal Parks and Gardens Dept. of the London Borough Council.

He enjoyed the outdoor life it suited him and as jobs went it was a good little number. There was a tidy bit of a pension at the end of it and he was looking forward to a comfortable retirement.

In the early years he often thought he might go home someday, but not now; going home was no longer an option. His life was here and anyway what was there to go home to? A few fields perched high on the side of a rainswept mountain. Fields that never grew anything but stones. The end of the road stopping a mile from the house with no shelter from the biting Atlantic winds. The roof of the old cottage would have fallen in by now. Best to forget it; going home was for younger men with people to go home to. Those thoughts were from another life; this was where he'd stay, there was no turning back.

He drained the last of the stout, picked up the paper and checked the evening racing. He put on a small bet every evening on the way home; nothing much, just a half-crown each-way. Sometimes he won, more often than not, he lost. If his selection obliged, he would buy the landlady a bit of a treat. A small box of fruity sweets or a bunch of flowers from the kiosk outside the bus terminal. Sometimes if she was ill, he'd get her a glossy magazine. Best of all she liked daffodils, and in the springtime, he always bought her those. She loved the deep yellow colour and the way the sunbeams through the windowpanes seemed to dance on the petals and light up the room. 'Yes,' he thought, 'all things considered, life had treated him kindly.'

He pulled an old silver fob watch from the pocket of his waistcoat and checked the time. Still two minutes left of his lunch break. The watch had been his fathers; he gave the face of it a polish on the front of his shirt before slipping it back in his pocket. He folded the paper and replaced it in his bag with his lunch box and the empty stout bottle. His wheelbarrow, rake and spade stood waiting, ready for the day's activity to continue. The sun was warm now and he thought it would make a nice evening. He hung the bag off his shoulder and bent to grasp the handles of the barrow. That's when he saw the man.

'Funny how I didn't notice him before,' he mused, 'I wonder what he's up to?'

The man was standing by some tall shrubbery, about fifty feet to the right of Jacob's position. He appeared to be staring into the middle distance and didn't appear to notice he was being observed. Jacob watched, taking in the man's overall appearance. He was an elderly man, tall, with a sort of military bearing. A very upright posture with his hands clasped behind his back gave credence to this theory. He had grey; almost snow-white hair where it wasn't covered by a brown trilby hat. A clipped military style moustache, under what Jacob would call an aristocratic nose, adorned his face. Despite the heat he wore a long, heavy, tan coloured overcoat more suitable for winter wear. His neck reminded Jacob of a turkey; thin and scrawny where it protruded above the collar of the snow-white shirt. The sun reflected off the gold pin that adorned the military type tie.

It was his eyes that held Jacob's attention; they seemed to cut right through him. Cold, penetrating eyes. The eyes of a predator. Eyes so black they seemed bottomless, yet they burned like fire. Beads of sweat broke out on Jacobs's forehead; he grasped the handle of his spade, his lips moved soundlessly in prayer and for the first time in his life he knew the meaning of real fear. These were the eyes of evil and Jacob McCarthy knew he was looking into hell.

His voice, when he found it, sounded like the croaking of a frog.

'Hey,' he shouted. 'The sign is there for a reason. It says keep off the grass. Can't you read?'

The man didn't answer, just gazed at him for a long moment from those unblinking eyes, before turning and walking into the shrubbery.

He felt the strength leaving his legs and he had to grab the seat to support himself as he struggled to regain his composure. He wiped the sweat from his brow and made his way to where the man had been standing.

The ground was soft here by the bushes, fresh from new digging. He'd only cleared this area two days previously and it had rained since, yet he noticed there were no footprints. Taking his courage in both hands he parted the bushes where the man had walked, nothing, an impenetrable wall of shrubbery.

'He must have gone that way' he thought, 'I saw him,' but there was nothing, no trace that he had ever been.

It puzzled him for the remainder of his working day and gave him a near sleepless night. Those eyes haunted his dreams.

The landlady commented on it the following morning.

'Perhaps you should have a lie in my dear,' she said, 'you don't look yourself at all. I could ring in and tell them your ill?

'No! Don't do that. It's nothing. I'll be alright.'

'Well if you say so.' She winked at him. Here was I living in hope, thinking we might be going back to bed. Jake McCarthy, you're one stubborn man.'

She waited by the front door and hugged him as he came out. 'You take it easy,' she said. 'Just slacken off for a day or so until your back in form. I've never seen you this way.'

'It's okay,' he said. 'Don't you worry.'

As he walked away, she shouted. 'I'll worry, of course I will. I'll never find a man again that would even come close to you.'

As he sat again on the park bench, going through the motions of eating his lunch, glancing through the paper but reading nothing, he was worrying enough for both of them, and though he would never admit it, he was afraid.

He felt the chill slowly at first, but gradually it enveloped his whole body. The hairs on the back of his neck stood to attention, seeming to have taken on a mind of their own.

Slowly, as if in the grip of mortal dread, he turned his head, the man was back, standing again in the same spot. His piercing gaze held Jacob rigid. Then he raised his right hand and in a motion that was nothing less than a command, he ordered Jacob to follow. He found he was powerless to resist. He followed the straight-backed marching figure down the path for a distance of maybe a hundred and twenty yards. Beads of cold sweat formed between his shoulder blades, and trickled slowly down to the small of his back. Then at the entrance to the maze, they stopped, the man looked back and their eyes locked. Jacob McCarthy looked once more into the depths of hell; then the figure faded from sight.

That night the landlady wanted to call in the doctor.

For the following three days the pattern was repeated. The figure of the man would appear every day at lunchtime; no words were exchanged the man would just gesture and Jacob, powerless to resist would follow. On each day the distance walked varied, but it was always further than the day before. No matter how fast he tried to walk the man was always twenty yards ahead of him. On the third day when the man stopped, Jacob reckoned they were probably half a mile from the park bench. They were standing by a large stand of old Elm trees due to be felled shortly as it was found they were diseased. This corner of the park had fallen into disuse and was for the main part, largely overgrown. Jacob knew that next year it would be his job to completely renovate it. To restore it once more to its former pristine condition. It was a challenge he was looking forward to, the last major project before retirement.

This time the man stared for a long time between the trunks of the giant Elms; his head moved slowly from side to side as if searching. Then he turned, looked once more at Jacob and pointed. He followed the direction of the pointing finger; when he looked back the figure had disappeared.

That night for the first time ever he only picked at his dinner, tried to make it appear as if he was eating something so as not to cause offence.

'What's the matter Jake? You look as though you've seen a ghost. You're very pale and you really do look quite ill.'

How could he explain to her that he thought he really

– 158 –

had seen a ghost?

'Look, skip dessert, even though it's your favourite, and get yourself to bed. A good night's rest is what you need. It'll do you the world of good.'

'Perhaps your right,' he answered, then by way of apology. 'I'm sorry I couldn't do justice to the dinner, put that desert in the fridge, I'm sure I'll enjoy it just as much tomorrow.'

'Oh Jake,' she said, 'I do worry, if anything should happen to you whatever would I do?'

I've told you not to worry, it's a thing of nothing it'll pass. He tried to sound cheerful. but his voice carried no conviction.

The following day the figure failed to appear. He was relieved at first, then puzzled. He skipped his lunch and decided he'd walk back to the area where he'd last seen the figure. As he walked his mind wandered. Thinking of the changes and improvements he could make in this place come the spring. He'd make it an oasis of colour where he could bring her on Sunday afternoons in the summertime. They could picnic there on the park bench and then lie out on the grass under the shade of that old Maple. She'd certainly enjoy that.

He reached the stand of Elms and went to where he thought the figure had been pointing. There didn't appear to be anything much to look at; nothing on the ground just the heavy fall of decomposing leaves from last autumn. They rustled now beneath his feet as he examined the tree trunks searching for clues. There was nothing.

'Well I couldn't have imagined it all, I definitely saw him.' It was some seconds, before he realised he was talking out loud. He walked through the whole stand of trees, then back to where he'd started. He was on the point of giving up and going back to work when the sun, obscured for a few moments behind a small white cloud, shone forth again in all its brilliance. Then he saw it, just by the side of the path, the sunbeams glinting off the gold. He stooped and picked it up, the last time he'd seen it was on the tie worn by the man. He turned it slowly between his fingers.

Jacob looked at the monogrammed gold tiepin. 'Now was he a ghost or not,' he mused. 'This pin seems real enough.'

He put the pin carefully in his waistcoat pocket next to his watch. He was just thinking that it might be worth a pound or two when he spotted something black protruding from the leaves. He kicked it in a kind of absent-minded manner, it didn't move but he heard something crack; the sound was like that of a breaking stick. He pushed back the leaves with the toe of his boot and his heart nearly stopped. The black object was a child's ankle-boot and a bleached white bone that he took to be a fragment of a leg was still encased in it. His kick had broken it at the ankle separating the foot from the shinbone.

His heart raced. Not being a man given easily to panic, he tried to gather his jumbled thoughts. There could be no doubt, it was a body. Worse than that it was the body of a child. He knew the procedures, go to the nearest telephone and call the police, that was the first rule. He covered the grisly find with leaves and walked as fast as he could to the storeroom where the phone was.

Half an hour later the park was closed to the public for the day. It became a crime scene. Police were everywhere.

He showed them where the body lay and was told sit in a police car and wait for further instructions. The stand of elm trees was fenced off with police barrier tape. Tents were erected and scene of the crime officers began to dig. Two hours later a young constable told him that a second body had been uncovered. The badly mutilated bodies were thought to be those of twin sisters missing for close on thirty-five years. Jacob was driven to police headquarters for questioning and the search continued.

The drive to the station at breakneck speed, with the siren screaming, shattered him. He was allowed to phone the landlady, but just to say he'd be helping police with their enquiries and would be delayed. There'd be plenty of time for explanations later.

He was ushered into a small room containing a small Formica topped table, with two chairs on one side and one on the other. Some sort of a recording device was on one end of the table. Two plainclothes officers took their places opposite him. The questioning began.

He told them all he knew. It wasn't a problem, remembering details. The whole incident had taken place over the duration of the previous week or so. After an hour they took a break and a policewoman brought him a cup of mediocre tasting tea from a dispensing machine in the hall. Then it started all over again, only much more aggressively the second time around.

A third officer joined them, a ratty, bad-tempered individual, who was in Jacob's face right from the off. The stink of whiskey coupled to his halitosis breath was nauseating.

'Ghost? Come again Paddy, you don't expect me to believe a cock-and-bull story like that. What fucking ghost?

What the fuck do you take me for?'

Jacob didn't answer.

'Are you fucking deaf as well as stupid Paddy? I'm talking to you, you thick Irish Mick.' No answer. 'Don't you fuck with me Paddy.'

Jacob looked at him, counted to ten slowly and spoke directly to the other two officers, totally ignoring Bad Breath.

'Before this charade goes any further my name is Jacob McCarthy not Paddy or Mick. I'll not answer any more questions until ye drop this asshole back into whatever sewer ye dragged him out of. Is that understood? If that can't be done, then I want a solicitor in attendance.'

Bad Breath gaped at him. 'Fuck me,' he sneered. 'It talks.'

'Not to you I don't.' Jacob retorted angrily. For the first time in as far back as he could remember he felt his temper bubbling just below the surface. He wanted to smash his fist into the face of this obnoxious idiot. After a five-minute recess the two officers came back alone.

This time he was just told to follow them. They took him upstairs to a long white painted room, a picture gallery. Enlarged black-and-white shots of the criminal fraternity hung at eye level on three of the walls. Some albums of photographs were produced; Jacob looked through them.

'Can you see the man you say you followed in any of these prints?' He couldn't. More albums followed but the man wasn't there. He stood up and was stretching himself and yawning when his eyes focussed on a picture by the door, he walked over for a closer look.

'That's the man,' he said. There was no mistaking the figure in the large monochromatic print. It was the man he had seen in the park.

Instantly the two officers sprang into full alert mode. Back in the interview room, this time with a smaller version of the photograph on the table between them, the questioning began again.

Jacob would never forget those eyes; there could be no doubt, it was the same man even if he was years younger when the picture was taken. The detectives spoke together, rapidly, in hushed tones. Jacob only caught a word here and there. They looked at him for a long time without speaking until at last one of them broke the silence and pointed at the photograph.

'You're absolutely sure this is the man you saw in the park?'

'Of course I am. He's a lot older than in your picture, but it's the same man. No doubt at all in my mind.'

He looked once more at the photograph. There was something... There it was the pin, the gold pin.

He rummaged in his waistcoat pocket, found the pin and laid it on the tabletop. 'He dropped this, I found it by the bodies, maybe it will help to identify him. I forgot about it until now but unless I'm very much mistaken it's the same as what's in that photo.'

It was. The monogrammed pin belonged to a Major Reginald Fortescue-Smyth.

'He was an ex-special forces intelligence co-ordinator, missing now for a quarter of a century or more. Suspected child abuser/molester, but with nothing ever proved. His wife disappeared a few years before he dropped off the radar, he was under suspicion for that too, but again with no real evidence.

The second detective took up the story.

'A very nasty piece of work, our Reggie, killer now as well it seems. If that bastard has surfaced again God help any kid who crosses his path. Child molesters they were called back then, it was too gentile a word for them. They're fucking paedophiles, plain and simple, it's a word much better suited to those bastards. The scum of the earth they are.'

He offered Jacob his hand, then by way of apology. 'Sorry for the inconvenience but you understand, it's procedure, we have to cover all bets. Thanks for your help with our enquiry sir. We'll be in touch if there's anything we need to clarify. Now, if you'll excuse us, I'll get one of our cars to drop you home.'

At the door he turned. 'Oh by the way, I seem to remember, it was a long time ago now, and I can't recall all the details, but I read somewhere that he had a child, a daughter, I think it was. She was brought up by her mother's people. There's not a great deal known about her, but her last known whereabouts were in the London area. It won't be very pleasant for her if that creep is lurking about again, what with all the media attention she'll be bound to attract. It'll be a proper nightmare. Well, I'll say goodnight sir, and thanks again.'

An unmarked car took Jacob home. He paused at the front gate noticing the light was still on in the upstairs bedroom. He went in as silently as possible, taking off his shoes and going quietly upstairs; the loose board on the landing creaked under his weight.

'Is that you Jake?' she called.

'Well I hope you're not waiting up for someone else,' he answered. They both laughed.

As he entered the room, he saw that she had been sitting up in bed, reading. 'This book you bought me is brilliant, I've never read anything so gripping,' she said. 'Do you remember, we watched the author being interviewed on the South Bank show a few months back?' He didn't.

'Never mind, get yourself back down those stairs. Your dinner is in the oven and pour yourself a whiskey. It'll do you good. When that's eaten get into this bed and tell me all about your day.' He did.

They talked long into the night; then they made love. At last totally sated they lay back in each other's arms.

'You're some man Jacob McCarthy,' she said. 'After the day you've had, and you can still turn in a performance like that. I was so lucky when you walked into my life. Can you just imagine what people will say when they hear that my Mr. McCarthy met a real live ghost?'

He was just on the point of nodding off to sleep when she spoke again.

'That chap you saw in the park, the ghost, Fortescue-Smyth? That used to be my name and I believe my dad used to be something in the military too. He was some sort of officer, a major, if I'm not mistaken. Probably just a coincidence, but strange just the same. My mother never spoke of him. In fact, I think she hated him. She left him soon after I was born. Then she vanished and I was brought up by her people.' She nibbled lovingly on the globe of his ear. 'Goodnight.'

Jacob lay there silently. Sleep eluded him. The events of the past week he turned over slowly in his mind. Going over everything he'd seen and recalling the words of the detective. Dawn was just streaking the sky with the first colours of daylight when he rose from the bed, a plan formulated, a decision made. He kissed the landlady lightly on the cheek and went to fetch his toolbox from beneath the stairs.

Early editions of London evening papers all carried much the same banner headline.

Two believed Dead in Mysterious Gas Leak in North London Suburb. *The occupants of the large, detached house in the leafy Blackheath Rd. area of North London are believed to be a female householder and a male lodger. They were believed to be the only occupants of the house at the time. Neighbours today described the couple as quiet, but friendly people who tended to keep to themselves. The man; believed to be an Irish citizen had been living in the area for a considerable number of years. He was believed to be in a relationship with the woman. Police sources say they and are not looking for anyone else in connection with the incident; believed to be a tragic accident. Further details will follow in our later editions.*

Several months later, on a sunny Thursday afternoon, Jacob's dream was inadvertently realized. In a ceremony attended by the Mayor of London, the local council and visiting dignitaries a new seat was unveiled in the corner of the park. Engraved on a small brass plaque was the inscription.

Erected by the London Borough Council
(Parks Division)
**In Memory of Jacob McCarthy,
'A Man for all Seasons.'**

The October Man

This was a part of town no one came to...

The late October rain spattered relentlessly on the steel-grey flagstones. I watched shivering, as it ran in torrents along the sides of the path. Debris of all sorts was carried from further up the street by the swiftly running dirty brown water. The drains and culverts long since closed up, in the aftermath of a long dry summer.

The rain now fell from a sky as black as ink. Thunder boomed, ear splitting, right overhead, before rolling across the city, almost in a never-ending rumble. Jagged forks of lightning flared briefly, ripping the darkness to shreds. Illuminating, for a few brief moments, the church steeple and the upper floors of the municipal buildings. The thunder now so loud it drowned out all other sounds.

I huddled in the deep-recessed doorway of what had once been the flagship store of a hardware and seed merchants. I pulled the collar of my jacket tight against the elements. The wind now driving the rain almost directly into the slight shelter afforded by the doorway.

'You wouldn't put a dog out in this,' I thought. Just then a dog of the large, nameless, hairy variety ambled by. Seemingly oblivious to the rain streaming off his long, unkempt sodden wet coat. The dog gave me a sidelong glance of total indifference from his sad old eyes as he cocked his leg, piddled against a lamppost and moved on. He disappeared into the gaping mouth of a laneway two doors further along.

There was very little passing traffic. An occasional car crawled slowly along the badly lit street, drivers watching for a whore desperate enough to brave the elements. The slow-moving wheels made waves in the rapidly rising flood-waters Water flowed across the path, into the depths of the doorway, soaking the legs of my trousers almost to the knees. This was a part of town no one came to, not without business; just winos and crackheads, and most of them wouldn't come this far out, preferring the sanctuary of the inner city.

Suddenly an explosion from further down the street, tore the humid air apart. A bolt of lightning found a target in a huge electric transformer. The already near dark street was plunged into total darkness. Leaving me helpless, temporarily blinded.

From the depths of the laneway came the blood-curdling screams of a startled cat, followed by the excited barking of the sad-eyed dog.

My heart seemed to miss a beat and a cold chill, started in the small of my back and danced a tango up the length of my spine. The eerie pitch-blackness enveloped the street like a shroud. Lightning flared again for an instant overhead, illuminating the doorway, bathing the faded posters on the glass-panelled door in an eerie white light. Everything from grass seed to rat poison was advertised there. I stumbled in the darkness and clutched at the door latch to prevent myself from falling. The latch clicked; the door creaked open on its rusty old hinges. Then with a loud squeal, swung inwards, carrying me with it. Totally unbalanced, I fell forward to lie prone on the rubbish-strewn floor of the shop.

I clambered to my feet, shaking and trembling. My throat dry, from the close contact with the dusty floor. I shivered, far more from the fright, then the cold. I stood without movement, waiting for my eyes to adjust to the gloom. God alone only knew what lay hidden and unseen in this place. What terror might lurk in the darkness?

Lightning flashed, showing me the layout of the gloomy interior. I saw a light switch on the wall near my shoulder, flicked it on, nothing happened. I checked the time, almost midnight. The storm raged on. Suddenly the streetlights flickered, and then went out again. A long minute passed, the lights flickered once more, then stayed on. A solitary bulb lit the dark and dusty interior of the shop. This was better at least I could see around a bit now.

The corners were still in total darkness. I could see that some old stock was still on the shelves. Dust, great thick layers of it was everywhere. A large grey rat scurried across the floor as a mouse ran down the length of the countertop. Cobwebs hung in profusion everywhere. Behind the counter, a trap door leading to a cellar stood ajar. On a shelf I found the burnt down stub of a candle and some matches; the first two matches refused to light, the third flared into life so unexpectedly I almost dropped it. My shaking fingers fumbled with the candle, finally getting the damp stub to ignite reluctantly. I dropped the still burning match, held the candle aloft and descended the cellar steps. Two steps from the bottom I stopped, and looked around, peering into the darkness.

Old packing cases were stacked haphazardly against one wall. The flickering candlelight cast shadows across the floor and on to the walls. The pale predatory eyes of a rat reflected the candlelight, as it followed my every move. A large black sheet completely covered another wall, draped like a curtain. I stepped carefully off the end of the stairs and crossed the floor, to stand before it; I reached out, grasped it and tried to pull it to one side. It fell from its hangings, collapsing in a cloud of dust. Spirals of dust hung in the air; caught in my throat and clogged my nostrils, making it difficult to breathe. I sneezed, lifted the candle, shining the dim light beyond where the curtain had been. That's when the nightmare began.

My legs buckled as I tried to stand upright; the blood froze in my veins and my eyes couldn't comprehend the horror of the scene before me. A vein throbbed in my temple, as my left eye, the one that always gave me trouble; twitched uncontrollably. This couldn't be happening, not to me, but it was.

Hanging from a crude wooden cross, in a parody of the Crucifixion was the naked body of a young woman. Her long dark hair was twisted around the wood of the cross, keeping her head upright. Her lifeless eyes stared vacantly right at me, through me, and on into the far corner of the cellar. A scream of the primal variety issued from deep down in my throat; a scream that numbed my senses and blotted out my reason. What in God's name had happened here?

A pentangle was drawn on the dusty floor, in front of the crucified body. The numbers 666 were clearly visible, scratched in the centre. The Mark of the Beast. This was clearly a ritualistic killing of some sort. The body had been split from crotch to breast, with what had obviously been a weapon of razor sharpness. Her entrails hung loose in a bloody mass from her body. A bloodstained knife lay on the ground at her feet. The blade pointing towards the centre of the pentangle. Blood dripped from her horrific abdominal injuries. It congealed in a bright red puddle on the cellar floor. I felt myself retching; emptying the contents of my stomach, to mingle with the victim's blood. Blood that looked black where the light didn't quite shine.

I slowly breathed in, breathed deeply, filling my lungs, forcing myself to stay calm. Trying to stay in control I counted to ten and then some. My mind raced, whoever did this could be anywhere in the building, concealed in the darkness, waiting.

I forced myself to look at the corpse, trying to keep my eyes averted from her injuries; she had been a good-looking woman, not anymore.

Suddenly, something flew right by my face, startling me. I shivered, feeling the chill of fear, but it was only a bluebottle disturbed by my intrusion and probably as scared as I was.

I looked up, clutched in the woman's right hand was a single long-stemmed red rose. The kind one saw hawked about the pubs and clubs at night, usually by young women of east European origin. My body convulsed and shook uncontrollably, as my eyes filled with tears. I sobbed. The tears ran down my cheeks as I fell to my knees, head bowed. The tears formed pools on the dusty floor, right in the centre of the pentangle. The Mark off the Beast swirled and blurred before my eyes, as my sobs subsided to a pitiful whimper. I knelt there for a long time before gathering myself together my thoughts in a turmoil. I noticed then that the thunder had stopped.

I rose slowly to my feet, attempting to brush the dust from my clothes and the palms of my sweat-soaked hands. The crudely fashioned cross with the corpse of the young woman had vanished, as had the pentangle. Of the Mark of the Beast, there was no sign. Turning to go, something caught my eye.

The long-stemmed red rose lay on the floor. A layer of grey dust covered its once crimson red petals like a shroud. Once the colour of blood, pulsating, vibrant as life itself, now the ashen grey of death.

I turned slowly, making my way up the creaking cellar steps to the store above. The black and purple storm clouds rolled towards a distant horizon. The dim light of a new dawn filtered through the last of the rain and the wind had died to a whisper. I snuffed out the last of the candle and exited on to the shiny wet pavement, breathing in the fresh damp air. The door clicked shut behind me and I stood there for a long moment, recovering my composure, lost in thought.

I had a good life, took pride in my achievements, some would say I was successful. Turning up my coat collar I shivered again. Someone had just walked on my grave. From across the street, high in the treetops, the dawn chorus burst into life.

Two streets away I found a news stand and an early morning breakfast bar; I ordered a coffee, found a seat and opened the paper. The headlines screamed across the front page.

Will the OCTOBER MAN strike again?

A sulky looking waitress brought the coffee, slopping it on the table as she set it down. She stopped to peer over my shoulder at the headlines.

'That guy must be mad,' she muttered. 'Totally insane.'

Mad? Insane? Was I hearing this? How dare she even think that way? How could she understand how good it felt to have power over life and death? Who else could show those unfortunate girls the road to true salvation? Surely there could be no more exalted a calling? Who or what gave this asinine idiot the authority to make such a sweeping statement?

The spectre in the cellar had been the first. Funny that, how she kept coming back year after year to my old store. Then this was Halloween, a time of ghouls and the ungodly. Who knew what might happen? Tonight, would be number seven. Lucky for some. I ran my thumb along the knife-blade in my jacket pocket, the edge honed to perfection. After all what was life for, but for dying?

I signalled the waitress for a refill. 'I still say that blokes insane. Mad as a hatter.'

Lock him up and throw away the key.'

I took the coffee and sipped at it. My eyes taking in every last detail of this painted Barbie, who would dare besmirch me, and belittle the nobility of my calling.

I smiled. Inside I boiled with a white-hot rage. Still smiling, I gazed into the eyes and stared at the heavily made-up face of my next lucky victim.

The Milkman

I never did fall off my bicycle again.

It was on a Tuesday. I know I'm right about that. I once asked my mother the same question, but I was about fifty years too late. She had no recollection at all. I was learning to ride a bike and falling off more often than staying upright. It was my big project at the time, learning how to balance and control an old bicycle someone had given my mother.

It was a great big black yoke and boy, did I hate it with a passion, but with the foolish exuberance of youth I was determined to master it, even if it was the last thing I did. On more than one occasion it very nearly was.

Every day on my way from school, I spent an hour with my nose Pressed against the big windows of the two bicycle shops. On one side of the street was Ned Murphys, directly opposite Ned Hankards. I divided my time equally between the two. Sometimes I ventured inside to try to get a better view of the gleaming, well-polished, chromed steel treasures on the window display. The mechanics didn't seem to mind, and the smell of grease and chain oil was like adrenaline in my veins.

Every day I vowed that come hell or high water, someday I was going to possess one of those machines. Where the not-so-small matter of the astronomical purchase price was going to come from didn't figure at all in the scheme of things.

Somebody once told me 'Have faith, God will provide.'

The only benefits bestowed on me were a multitude of cuts and multi-coloured bruises. Mind you, he did listen to me. Every time I asked to give me a break, He very nearly did, but a broken arm, a dislocated shoulder or a shattered knee were never too far up on the list of my priorities.

I'd hit the ground so often my forehead was like a cobblestone street.

Me and whatever God was doing duty, seemed to have our wires crossed as to what constituted a break, so eventually I gave up bothering him.

I was half sitting, half lying on the ground cursing yet another mishap, and squeezing my eyes tightly shut to hold back the tears. Not tears from my latest conflict with gravity, but from my own inability to tame that great black brute that was now lying across me. A brake handle was stuck in one nostril, while a pedal was attempting to ensure that I'd talk in a high-pitched voice and walk with a wiggle for the rest of my life. I had a vision of my mother laughing herself sick at the idea of deleting the R off the end of my name.

A miracle happened that day that probably changed the course of my life.

I heard footsteps approaching. I felt rather than saw myself being untangled from the bike. Tentatively I opened one eye for a peep. A man wearing a long blue shop coat, was placing my bike carefully against a wall. Then he caught me under both arms and lifted me to my feet. It was the milkman.

'Are you okay?' He asked.

I nodded slowly as the dizziness passed and his face came into focus.

'Come with me.' He said. 'Your old bike will be safe enough where it is, and you'll be a whole lot safer without it.' He clapped me on the back, tousled my hair and chuckled.

'Don't worry lad, you'll learn to ride it soon enough.'

At that particular moment I was hoping I'd never set eyes on the damn thing again.

'Come on.' He said. 'How does a cup of tea and slab of homemade apple pie sound? The missus has the kettle boiling and she won't mind if there's one extra.'

He took me into his house and introduced me to his wife. Tea was poured and a large slice of hot apple pie accompanied with a huge dollop of whipped cream found its way onto my plate.

He told me about his job. Delivering milk from door to door. He'd built up a big round and he was thinking of taking on an assistant. He'd discussed it with his wife and as the lad who'd held the job was departing the following week, would I be interested? Would I? It was as if the clouds had parted and a sunburst flashed before my eyes. Here, in one fell swoop was the answer to my problems. Without even thinking about what might be involved, I agreed. Then, as if he'd been discussing things with an adult, he told me what would be expected of me and what I could expect in return.

I would have to start at seven and deliver to the forty or so houses in our area on my own. He'd collect me at eight and I'd help him until nine, then he'd deliver me to school. On Saturdays we'd work until lunchtime and on Sundays the round was considerably shorter, so we'd be finished about eleven.

For this (and he consulted his notebook and got a nod of agreement across the table from his wife) I'd get the sum of two pounds and five shillings a week and at Christmas I'd receive a five pound note as a bonus.

My eyes must have been like saucers. A five-pound note; this was an absolute fortune.

I was (in my own mind) after hitting the big time and in those few minutes I grew about a foot. Then he added an appendage. Two pounds a week would be given to my mother and I would receive five shillings. Also when I was old enough he'd teach me to drive.

Bicycles suddenly lost their allure. My imagination went into overdrive so fast I nearly had a burnout.

'Are you agreeable?' He asked.

I was so agreeable I'd have left him adopt me. He closed his dog-eared old account book, then (in the way of country people) he spat on his palm and put out his hand to seal the deal. All of a sudden being a big boy must have gone to my head. I tried to do the same, missed, and left a big dribble of spit down the front of his coat. Years later he told me that his wife laughed so much over that incident, he thought he'd be drawing down the life insurance.

I spent four very happy years riding shotgun for the milkman. No denying, it was hard work in all weathers, but I don't think I ever missed a day. I got an education in human nature that I'd never have got otherwise. I learned about handling money and how to tell the difference between truth or lies as some customers could really spin a yarn.

The milkman for his part, more than lived up to the agreement. Twice a year he'd take me to McMahons shoe shop to be fitted with a pair of strong leather shoes. When the time came for him to purchase a new van, he took me with him and asked my opinion.

'As you're going to be spending as much time in it as I am, we might as well get something that suits us both.'

That was the sort of man he was.

I never did get a new bike. Six months later my father found me a second-hand one. A multi-speed racer, Bright green. I paid off the three-pounds purchase price at ten shillings a week.

Did my life change course the day I met the milkman? I like to think it did. I was very lucky in that I met a very decent man who looked out for me. He never once pointed me in a wrong direction. He instilled in me a serious work ethic that served me well throughout my working life.

Jim Moriarty, wherever you are now, I can only salute you and say thanks to a man in a million.

I never did fall off my bicycle again.

The Halloween Encounter

If that woman had to make soup from a stone...

The elderly man climbed stiffly from the high wooden bar stool and drained the last dregs of beer from his glass; then he held it to the light, as if by some miracle, there might still be some remaining. His luck was out, it was empty. He glanced around the small public bar. There was no generosity on the faces of the patrons. He'd have tried for one on credit if Alice the barmaid had been there, but against the boss he stood no chance. There was so much on the slate he reckoned they'd run out of chalk. 'Well,' he thought, 'I reckon it's time I wasn't here.' He slipped out the side door of the Silver Fox.'

'You be careful out there, Zak' somebody called after him. This was followed by a guffaw of laughter. The man didn't answer.

'Buffoons,' he thought. Let the buggers laugh, someday it'll be my turn.'

He felt the first sporadic drops of rain on his grizzled features as a bat flew out of the beam of a streetlight and whizzed by his face. He stood for a minute taking in his surroundings, waiting for the unexpected, watching for the unseen, listening to the silence. At last, satisfied that he was alone, he went to his hiding place in the hedge. He probed with his hand, cursing under his breath when a thorn from a long dead dog rose pricked his thumb. His hand closed on the well-worn stock of his old shotgun. He withdrew it carefully from the brambles and then extracted his bag with

– 181 –

the box of cartridges, two crumpled cheese sandwiches, an apple and a small flask. He'd have liked it fine if the flask contained whisky, but that only happened in dreams. Tea was a poor second choice, but beggars don't get to choose.

He gave a long low whistle and a crossbreed dog emerged from under the hedge and rubbed against his leg. He patted the dog's head and glanced back with a wistful expression at the welcoming beam of yellow light showing through a chink in the curtains of the bar. Going back was not an option. 'Ah well.' He muttered to himself. 'When needs must, the Devil drives.'

He shivered and crossed himself, thinking it wouldn't do to invoke evil on a night the ungodly were said to walk the earth. Halloween didn't frighten him, but it was as well not to take chances. The forces of darkness were better left to themselves.

'Come on boy,' he said, as he hefted the bag on to his shoulder, tucked the shotgun under his arm, and clinging to where the shadows were deepest, set off on his quest. The dog, Gypsy, plodded at his heels.

Isaac Malone, or Old Zak as he was better known, was a man endowed with a deep knowledge of wild herbs, plant life and their benefits to the wellbeing and health of his fellow men. He was also a poacher of note. He had once been a gamekeeper, as had his father, grandfather and probably back further than that. But the estate was sold off and his services were no longer required. His years were against him getting any chance of employment elsewhere, so he just took to poaching. After all it was what he'd being doing legally all his life. He hoped for a few pheasants tonight, and who knows, if he was lucky, maybe a small deer.

The cold of the rain reached into his bones; making him wish he was at home. Tucked up in bed in the old attic room over the kitchen, snuggled up to his treasure, Molly his much loved wife.

He thought of her fondly. She was a tough old bird, but by God she knew how to warm a man. It was a long time now since the gypsies had camped out by the woods, near the bend in the river. That's where he'd first seen her.

He remembered it now like it was yesterday, the flickering firelight reflecting off hair as black as the feathers of a crow and dancing in the ebony of her eyes. Her father had driven a hard bargain. That sweet little piebald pony he'd just finished training was the price, but she had never given him cause to regret it. Her looks were going now as hardship and age took its toll, but she was still all woman, with a dignity and beauty that were all her own. She was always loyal and never moaned when the pickings were meagre. She just made the best of it. If that woman had to make soup from a stone, it would taste just fine. They had never been blessed with children, but he accepted that as being a cross to bear.

'If I do well tonight,' he thought, 'I'll get her a new winter coat, a red one and a nice silver brooch to pin on it.' He plodded on driven by his desire to please her and the need to let her know she was loved.

By the time he reached the crossroads he was feeling the dampness through his clothes. He was on the point of going home when he saw the outline of a girl silhouetted against the dim light of the rising moon. He thought he recognised her and was on the point of calling out a greeting when he heard the sound of a car approaching.

It was travelling fast. 'Too fast for these roads and weather conditions,' Isaac thought. 'Probably one of those young bucks from the town.'

In the lights he saw the girl stick her thumb out; the car slowed, then skidded on the wet surface as the brakes were applied. As the girl got in, she looked towards him, it was Alice, the barmaid from the Silver Fox.

They'd been talking in the pub early on how some young girl went missing from these parts a few Halloweens past and was never seen again. But she was from over Northwood direction and that was maybe twelve miles away.

'Anyway,' he thought, lightning doesn't strike twice.' He liked Alice, she was a good 'un, always treated him right. They had a code between them, him and Alice. If he called a half, it meant he had no money. She'd slip him one. When he called her on the pretext of paying, she'd suddenly go deaf.

He found the spot where the wall was tumbled and clambered over the moss-covered stones. He felt his old bones ache with the effort.

'I'll not be able to do this for more than another year or so,' he thought, 'God only knows what will happen to us then?'

High in the branches an owl hooted giving warning of his approach. The moonlight filtered through the leafless branches, casting eerie shadows all about. The woodland paths were strewn with leaves, but they barely rustled beneath his feet as he passed. The dog gave a low growl of warning, as a slow-moving badger scurried back to his set at their approach. 'Good boy Gyp,' he whispered, 'Shush now.

He'd reached a clearing between the trees when the thunder started. He counted off the seconds. He'd just reached two when a jagged streak of forked lightning seemed to split the sky and bathed the clearing in an electric blue luminescence. He heard the crash of falling timber from where he guessed the lightning must have struck.

'Only a mile or so east,' he thought. 'But moving away, best wait...'

He never finished what he was thinking; an unearthly ear-splitting scream mingled with the sound of the rolling thunder.

Isaac's blood froze, the dog whimpered and cowered, shivering at his feet. He crouched and patted the dog and crossed himself again.

'Whatever that was Gyp my lovely,' he thought, 'It wasn't of this world.'

He debated what to do. Whatever might be said about him, there wasn't a man alive that could call him a coward. With a silent apology to his dog he decided to investigate.

He'd been brought up in these woods. He'd had his education here, and he could find his way around blindfolded. He placed the direction the scream had come from and hesitated, Satan's Meadow.

Legends, told of blood sacrifices and Satan worshipping, going back to time immemorial. It was said that the Devil himself walked there on Halloween. It always gave Zak an uneasy feeling. Not a place to be after dark. The bag he concealed between the roots of an old oak and loaded his gun; using the heavier charge he would need for deer.

He walked cautiously; overhead the thunder still boomed, but less frequently. There was now ten seconds or more between the lightning flashes. Every few minutes he stopped to get his bearings. The dog walked tight against his heels.

He pulled out his watch and waited, the lightning flashed, and he checked the time. Eleven minutes to midnight, still a way to go. He increased his pace. The path was almost overgrown. Dead tree branches concealed in the undergrowth caused him to stumble. Brambles caught in his clothes and tore at his hands. Heavy drops, falling from the leaves now soaked him to the skin.

He tried to remember what he knew of the Hollow; it wasn't much, three slabs of stone arranged into a crude altar in the centre of what was a natural amphitheatre. Archaeologists had once dated some artefacts found there back to 10000 B.C. Outside of the half-cocked legends, as far as he remembered, no one had ever shown any interest in the place since.

He was silently cursing his stupidity for coming here when the dog emitted a low warning growl. The dog crouched low to the ground; hackles raised, ready to spring, when Zak heard the voices.

It wasn't a song as such; more of a chant, and he didn't recognise the language. It was accompanied by a rhythmic thumping on some sort of drum. It was coming from just beyond the trees, straight ahead. He crept forward, noting now that the dog was growling continuously. He dropped to his knees and crawled the last few yards, before looking down on his objective. He rubbed his eyes with his free hand to make sure he wasn't seeing things. The sight before him was incredulous. He looked away, then looked back again, but everything was as he had thought.

Torches burned around the grassy hollow illuminating the bizarre scene. The flickering flames cast shadows across the faces of the black-robed chanting throng. Spread-eagled across the old stone altar was the naked body of Alice from the Silver Fox. She wasn't moving and he couldn't tell if she was still alive, but the creature wearing the antlers of a deer and rutting with her comatose body certainly was. As the creature climaxed, the volume and tempo of the drumming increased, the chanting reached a crescendo, then suddenly stopped.

The silence in the hollow was eerie, the audience disrobed, waiting, the tension in the air was palpable. Steadily falling rain glistened like silver sequins on the naked bodies of the watchers. The creature climbed from the altar and stood facing the audience. He was handed a long-bladed knife. The grotesque mask hiding his features sent shivers up Isaac's spine. If there really was a devil, this thing before him was surely it.

He fingered the small gold cross he wore. It had been a gift from his Molly and since the day she'd fastened it around his neck, it had never been taken off. A few times since it was the power of that cross that had brought him to safety; of that he was certain.

The creature began to chant a long incantation; he seemed to be trying to invoke a response from an unseen watcher. The hypnotic chanting stopped. The drum beat slowly. With the knife, clasped in both hands, the creature raised it above the breasts of the unconscious girl. Suddenly he screamed a warning, pointing straight at Isaac.

There was a flurry of movement to Isaac's right. From the corner of his eye he saw the black form of Gypsy leap through the air, grasping the wrist of a would-be assailant. He heard the crunch of bones and the scream of a woman. Down in the hollow the intentions of the creature were unmistakable. Alice was going to die.

Zak squeezed the trigger and the head of the beast exploded in a red mist. The fine spray of blood mingled with the drizzling rain. The headless corpse stood for a moment, then the knife slipped from its lifeless fingers. It collapsed across the form of the girl, spouting blood formed a pool of gore between her naked breasts. He discharged the second barrel into the air, the loud boom adding to the chaos as the crowd in the arena panicked and scattered. The black clad woman at his feet moaned and stirred. The dog growled, she pleaded for mercy, there was none. Zak thumped her hard on the forehead with the butt of the shotgun, causing her to lose all interest in the proceedings.

It was long after the last of the watchers had left the Hollow. The woods were once more shrouded in silence, before he moved. The torches were all but burned out, barely flickering now in the pre-dawn mist. The first grey streaks of dawn would soon be painted on the sky, the first colours of a new day.

He walked to the altar. The disciples had taken the corpse of the man-beast. The blood was almost washed from the body of the girl. Crimson rivulets trickled from her sides onto the wet grey slab of the altar stone.

She was conscious now, but too frightened to move, shivering uncontrollably, in deep shock as the memory of the trauma began to take effect. He helped her to stand, then pulled off his rain-soaked coat and covered her as best he could. He found some discarded shoes and put them on her feet, they were too big but at least she could walk; as he knelt to fasten them, he saw the bag.

It was a black leather briefcase. Expensive, like someone of importance might own. He clicked the locks, and it sprang open. His eyes popped for the second time that night. It was crammed full of large denomination bank notes. If there was an ill wind, it had certainly blown him some good. the answer to his prayers. He smiled wryly.

'Molly my girl, you're finally going to get a pay-day you richly deserve.' he thought.

Supporting the weight of the girl with one hand and clutching the briefcase and the gun in the other, they walked slowly out of the arena. From high in the bare branches of a dying elm, the malignant eyes of a large black crow followed their every move; then it swooped to view the body of the woman beneath the trees.

Waste not, want not. It pecked at the wide staring eyes. Almost finished, it screamed, the sound almost sorrowful. It pecked one last time, then flew silently high above the treetops, into the low grey clouds.

Days Like This

Bang! Whoever it was would have the door off the hinges

We've all had them; days that are etched in our thoughts and destined never to be forgotten. Hidden in our memories, they lie there dormant, waiting in ambush; catching us when we're most unwary. These are the days that now and then break through the flimsy disguise of our facade to remind us that life never runs quite as smoothly as we would foolishly like to believe.

As days go, the day as it started, seemed normal enough, but by the time I got my ten o'clock tea-break the wind had changed and what's it that's said of an ill wind...? That day it certainly blew me no good.

Somewhere between the big breakfast roll and the last dregs of tea, I asked the question. 'Lads! Does anybody know a plumber that might be interested in doing a small job?'

The reply, if there was one, was lost amongst sniggers, raised eyebrows and shrugged shoulders. Didn't I know that this was Celtic Tiger Land? Plumbers didn't do small jobs anymore. I'd have a better chance of winning the lottery three weeks in a row than of getting a plumber to do a small job.

As we trooped from the canteen, amidst the stamping and shuffling of feet, I was lead to understand that plumbers were important people. From what I could gather; most of them did their Saturday night socialising in places like Marbella.

'Small job?' One wit laughed derisivly. 'Forget it Olly. Those days are long gone. It's never going to happen, mate.'

Oh! That he could have been so right.

But scarcely an hour had passed before the wind changed. I was in the company store when a hand descended on my shoulder. It was a hand that exerted the pressure of a clamp and forced me to look upwards. A button that was positioned about midway on someone's shirt was looking straight back at me. I looked further up and from about a yard above me, a face akin to a full moon, beamed down on me.

'How's it going there boy?' asked the giant, then with the next breath, answered his own question. 'You're well.'

I nodded in agreement; nodded as much as the pressure on my shoulder would allow. Who was this guy? I wasn't long in finding out.

'You're the fellow that's looking for a plumber? Am I right?'

I was about to nod again when the clamp was removed from my shoulder. Before I could muster a reply, he answered for me. 'Look no further boy. I'm your man.'

'Excuse me for asking, but who exactly are you?' I asked timorously as I waited for my collarbone to click back into place.

He told me. I didn't know him, though he assured me I should. 'Aren't I from the same place as yourself?'

I'd never seen him before in my life. Shrugging the shoulder that still remained intact, I said, 'I've no idea.'

'Ah never mind. Once seen never forgotten, isn't that the way of it? Now what's this job you might want doing?'

'Are you a plumber?' I asked.

Obviously it was a stupid question, for it earned me a look of complete derision that almost withered me.

'Plumber? You're asking am I a plumber? Listen to me boy, anyone will tell you; I'm the best plumber in Ireland.'

Who was I to argue? If the rest of them were whooping it up in Marbella; maybe he was.

It being the easiest thing to do, I capitulated and told him what I had in mind. If he'd asked for it I'd have given it to him in writing. In a voice that boomed with confidence he assured me.

'It's a thing of nothing, ten minutes in and out. Job done.' He said we should shake on it and I staggered away wondering should I call South Doc or go directly to A&E.

It was a couple of weeks later, just a day or two before Christmas '97 when the wind really did change and for the worst. In the early hours of the morning it started and the country was lashed all day long by hurricane force winds. Hardly a house was left untouched such was the extent of the damage. Power lines collapsed and slates tumbled from rooftops like some deadly confetti. Trees fell like dominos causing traffic chaos right across the lenght and breadth of the country.

I was at home thanking my lucky stars that the roof wasn't in the garden when the power went off. Ah well! These things happen. I wasn't too badly off. There was a good fire down and within five minutes the previous years Christmas Candle was once more doing duty and casting a warm glow around the living room. My mother was asleep in armchair by the fire and all was well in my corner of the world. What a foolish assumption.

Someone pounded on the front door, whoever it was

had no notion of going away. That ill wind blew stronger than ever.

Some worse-case scenarios flashed before me and I dismissed them all but one; it had to be a neighbour in trouble. I looked out on a day as black as night. It was still only four o'clock.

Bang! Whoever it was would have the door off the hinges. **Bang! Bang! Bang!** I answered it. The face looking down at me was familiar; full moon sprang to mind. Oh no! This was a scenario I hadn't even imagined. One I'd completly forgotten. 'How's it going? I was in the area so I thought I might as well as do that little job for you.'

'Couldn't it wait until the New Year?' I plucked up the courage to suggest. 'The weather isn't exactly favourable.'

'Ah New Year be damned! We might all be dead by then. What's the weather got to do with it? Sure isn't it an inside job, I'm here now, so let's be getting on with.'

This guy didn't know how to take no for an answer. Blissfully unaware, my mother snored on. We circled each other like prize-fighters until I threw in the towel and defeated, led the way to the kitchen. 'This is what I want done,' I said. 'Move the sink from underneath the window to the gable wall.'

'No bother. As I said, a ten minute job. I'll just get the gear from the van.'

'I'd better show you where the stop-cock's located,' I said. He stopped in mid-stride and fixed me with such a look of disdain I wished there was a hole I could crawl into and hide.

'You don't know much about the plumbing game, do you?'

I had to confess. 'Nothing'

'I'm a professional. No need for anything like that. That kind of thing is only for amateurs. No worries, it's in safe hands.'

'You mean you're not turning off the water at the mains?'

'That's what I just said, wasn't it?

Doubt about the abilities of my choice of plumber didn't just creep in; they galloped. A Derby winner couldn't run faster than my brain was revolving. Two minutes later he was back; armed with an adjustable wrench, a hacksaw and a coil of pipe.

'Right! Here's what we're going to do. As you can see I've fitted a valve on the end of this pipe. When I cut through the live line you slap the valve down on the pipe and hey presto, job is three-quarters done.'

'But there will be water...' I protested feebly.

'Ah just a cupful. Nothing to worry about. Are ye ready?'

It sounded simple, but I'd read The Readers Digest guide to D.I.Y and one thing the Editorial stressed was always turn off the water before commencing a job. Still the guy said he was professional; didn't he?

'Right! Here we go.' He cut. Like a cat waiting to pounce, I crouched and waited. *Hiss-sss-ss-s.* Water seeped for a fraction of a second, then all hell broke loose. The pipe parted and water at the force of an Icelandic geyser hit me in the eye. I dropped the valve and ran for cover while at full throttle water blasted off the kitchen ceiling. The Christmas Candle, sputtered and went out. The plumber tripped over the pipe and re-directed the stream of water out through the kitchen door and across the sitting room. It ran down the curtains and across the floor. The commotion woke my mother and in minutes she was ankle-deep in water that was rising rapidly.

Eventually we got it stopped but the ground floor could have been declared a disaster area. It was like a lake. Everything in sight had been thoroughly soaked. How did we stop the deluge? We turned the water off at the stop-cock; that's how.

The man with the Full-Moon face surveyed the flood. 'We've a small drop of water, but what of it? Be thankful to God there's no harm done. Just open the back door and most of it will go down the garden, The rest of it will dry up in no time.'

The ten minute job was now gone over half-an-hour and the sink still wasn't in position. An hour later after much pulling, tugging, and at times prolific bouts of swearing, the job was completed in a kind of a way. That is to cover the distance of about a yard and a half he used about thirty yards of piping. How did he manage that? From the work-top to the ceiling and back again he ran the pipe like the bellows of a concertina. The word mess doesn't even come close to describing it.

My mother was on the verge of hysterics. I was thinking I'd have to get her sedated. No need, she was laughing. Laughing fit to burst. Women! She thought the whole thing was hilariously funny. Me! I was ready to kill and just hoped she'd kept the insurance policy up to date.

The plumber sloshed his way to the door. He beamed down at me, but such was the redness of the Full-Moon face it now more closely resembled Mars.

'Don't worry about my bill. You'll be getting mates rates, but we'll sort that out in the New Year; enjoy the Christmas.'

I was too gob-smacked to reply before the door slammed. It nearly caused a tidal wave. He actually expected to get paid. Think again, I thought, it's never going to happen. My mother laughed on as I surveyed the catastrophe. I'd probably have cried, but it would have only risen the water level.

Think. I did. It looked like only the man for lost causes could rescue me from this one. Out of earshot of my mother, I muttered. 'Hey St. Jude get me out of this and I'll bang a fiver in the post for you.'

Long silence. 'What d'ye say?' I prompted him. I was about to give up when the answer finally came through. 'You will yeah? What happened the last fiver? Oh yeah! And don't forget the one before that?'

'Okay! Okay! Don't be confusing me. This time I'll make it ten. Now get on with it. I'm drowning here.'

True to form he came up trumps, but then he always does.

Simple! Why hadn't I thought of it myself. The solution was surely in the Golden Pages. Things began to look a little brighter.

'Hello! Hello! McCarthy's plumbers? Hello, is anybody there?' The line went dead. I tried again. This time a different number. 'Hello! Is that the 24 hour Plumbing Service? Hello! Hello! can you hear me?'

Ah! Success. This time; an answering machine.

'Hello! Hello! When you get back from Marbella I've a big job need seeing to...'

The Death of Life

Ellen Reilly - 4th Febuary 1890

The day that I asked myself the first questions was a bright sunny afternoon. That was the day I first visited the cemetery of St. Joseph. Something drew me here to this place; I've passed this way plenty of times and never noticed it, what was so different about today? Why did I come here? That's a question along with many others I have no answer for. What had caused me to stop and investigate the solitude of a lonely country cemetery?

I didn't intentionally set out to come here just when passing on the road I was struck by the serene beauty of the place, It could have been a scene that Constable might have painted, had he stood where I was standing at that time. The myriad shades of colour, mostly green, going through the whole gamut of the spectrum. Here Grey might have been inspired to write his Elegy if he'd sat on the bench beneath the yew trees of an evening.

The first thing that caught my eye were the horses, a bay and a chestnut. From the boundary ditch of the field they stood watch over this oasis of tranquillity. Nuzzling each other now and again almost like lovers on a tryst. They might have stepped from a canvas of George Stubbs. Here in their demesne I was the intruder.

The black iron gates hung on stone-built pillars, I read the inscription. St. Josephs Cemetery. A place, where the destitute were interred in the years gone by. Those poor impoverished ones whose circumstances did not deem them worthy of a place on hallowed ground. Such was the thinking of 19th century Irish Catholicism. It might not have been that way everywhere. It was certainly that way in East Cork.

The absence of gravestones struck me as odd. There was only the one, barely visible above the high grass. I took a closer look, a few yards further on was a second one, even smaller than the first but only one bore an inscription.

Ellen Reilly,

4th Feb. 1890,

aged 30 years.

The date this woman had died on was the same month and day as my daughter was born three quarters of a century later. Was it just a coincidence or was it fate moving mysteriously?

Who were youEllen Reilly? How did you come to be in this place? Did our paths cross somewhere in another life? Was it merely a century ago or further back through the ages of time? It wasn't an accident, I'm sure of that. No! I was meant to pass this way, meant to find you, for whatever reason.

I wondered about you and your journey here to this place. It had to be lonely. Lying in the plain rough-hewed timber box lined with sawdust and wood shavings swept from the floor of the carpenter's workshop.

Just five weeks after your last Christmas, it must have been cold. Did you cook a Christmas dinner for your husband and children, not realising it would be for the last time? I think not, on Christmas Day of 1889 you would have been on the breadline.

What caused your demise? Did you die of consumption or in childbirth or was your death from the deadliest of all diseases? That of poverty.

The merchants of Midleton would, no doubt, have attended to business as usual. The doors of shops and public houses would not have closed, as the horse pulling the cart with your remains passed slowly up the street. They wouldn't have doffed their hats as you went by or given a thought to your demise. If you were coming to this place, you would have been considered a person of no consequence.

Women standing about at the gates of the butter market might have nudged each other, asking as to who you were. They wouldn't have really cared; it was just to make idle gossip. Your passing would be seen as an interruption to the important business of the day.

The freshness of the produce hanging above the barrels of salted fish would be checked, before a decision was taken on the price of a few eggs and a loaf of bread.

This was important, this was about life, and in the year 1890 it would have been about survival. Selecting a half-head, a few crubeens and a head of cabbage was business of some importance. About you, Ellen Reilly dead and a pauper nobody would have really cared.

I know a priest would have accompanied the cart carrying your remains to the spot where the rail-line crosses the road. Then with duty done you'd be left alone. Would he have come to wish you well on your journey and sing your praises in a final and fitting eulogy? No! The dignity of such a gesture would not be wasted on you, or any of those that found rest in this place. The black clad man would have returned to the comfort of his fireside on a cold evening in early spring, rather than to walk here with you?

Was it raining that day? The cold wet drops falling on the heads of those that mourned you. Altered forever by your passing, would be the lives of your heartbroken parents. Had you siblings that would have walked out from the town behind you? Shedding tears that mingled with the raindrops on their faces.

Maybe it was snowing. Like a white mantle it would have come from the northwest and blown across the fields, falling on the heads of those that followed your procession to pay their last respects and giving them the appearance of Wraiths. The footprints and wagon tracks would be covered leaving no trace of your last sad journey. Up there on the hill, from behind the windows of Ballyedmond House lights would have flickered and twinkled? Snowflakes would take on the appearance of dancing in a kaleidoscope of whiteness. Would anybody watching from the shadows of an upstairs room have muttered a prayer as you passed on the road below and wondered about your life?

Behind would come those tasked with filling in your grave beneath the beeches. They would be the ones who stamped down the cold, wet earth over your remains. For a few glasses of porter and a naggin of cheap whiskey, any sign that you ever existed would be buried forever. Leaving nothing behind to remind people that you had ever lived, laughed, cried or loved. Dying was easy, living was the hard part.

But on the *4ᵗʰ of February 1890* here in this field of the forgotten, somebody did care about you *Ellen Reilly; someone* thought enough of you to erect a stone to your memory. Now a century and a quarter later those who thought themselves above you are unknown; no one else is remembered here but you. Whoever chose this place, chose it well. The colours of the setting sun give this place the light and luminosity of a Turner watercolour, for it too was surely created by the hand of a master. When autumn comes the leaves on your grave will shine like burnished copper giving a well-deserved richness to your resting place.

What brought me to stand by your grave? Something did. It was as if a bond between us drew me here, but it's something else that remains unanswered.

The great house on the hill is gone for half a century now, there is nothing left but some moss-covered stones on the headlands, most having been ploughed beneath the fields on the hillside. There are few people around Midleton today who would remember it ever existed, but you; your name crudely chiselled on a simple limestone marker in a small field in Broomfield West will be remembered for eternity.

High above the landscape of East Cork, a crescent moon hung suspended in a cloudless night sky. I watched as it danced with the stars. The chestnut mare whinnied softly, alarmed at the silent approach of a fox, moving stealthily through the long grass of the meadow. The fox stopped, lifted his head and sniffed the air before altering his route by a fraction. The slight breeze that rustled through the leaves on the beeches whispered a lullaby to placate those that rest here. It murmured soothingly in harmony with my prayer for the souls of those that inhabit this place.

Someday when my remains are scattered here; will you be waiting? Standing there in the shadows by those black iron gates. Who knows? I have questions; I believe you may have answers.

My Father

I didn't need a hero, the one I had was bigger and better than any

I t took me years, a lot of years, not just to become an
adult but to grow up. Years of being a teenager, full of
angst, that those years bring. Not for one minute caring
that other people existed, besides me. I was the one, the
great be all; the world as I knew it should revolve around
me. It's easy to see now, looking back, how naive I was, if
stupidity was a crime... I'd be guilty as charged.

One of my earliest memories and the very first time I'm
sure I would ever have picked up a paintbrush was when we
lived on an estate near county Limerick. Lough Gur. It was
one of the oldest Celtic settlements in the country.

The house we lived in, went with the job. One day my
father was painting the roofs of hay-barns when I got the
foolish notion of lending a hand. While he was shifting lad-
ders, I robbed the bucket of tar and made my way to the
big house. I had designs worthy of Picasso decorating the
the walls near the front door before I was apprehended.
All hell broke loose. The woman of the house dropped all
pretensions of being a lady and cursed me as roundly as she
could. By all accounts her prolific use of profane language
was something never heard in that part of the county before and earned her a dubious moment of fame.

My father spent the best part of a week trying to oblib-
erate my very first effort at a piece of artwork. It was years
later before I discovered that my 'crime' had cost him his

job and lost us our house. A patient man. He never once showed anger or raised a hand against me.

There were four of us in family, two boys and two girls. I became a teenager in nineteen sixty-one. I've no recollection of the actual day. A lot of years have rolled past the door since I blew the candles out on my thirteenth birthday cake. I woud have got a cake; nothing is more certain, my father would have seen to that.

It was the sixties. If he thought during those formative years, that I was the spawn of the devil; who could blame him. I never seemed able to make a right turn.

It was the era of the cold war, the Cuban missile crisis, rock 'n' roll and euphoria about the Beatles. More than any other it was the decade that changed the course of peoples lives. Television became a reality. Man first walked on the moon. It was when an assassin's bullet took the life of John F. Kennedy on a street in Dallas Texas, on a sunny afternoon.

I well remember my father listening to the news bulletins on a big brown Pye radio that took pride of place in the corner of our kitchen. He'd sit in front of that set and hang on every word. It was the news event of the day, the year, and probably the decade. People still talk about it, over half a century later. It was the dream of the news media, stories just didn't come any bigger. For the most part it passed us by.

That old radio was like a lifeline to another world. He loved to listen to anything he could. Every eveningwas the program he liked most of all. The Archers. The long-running saga of a farming family in Ambridge, a fictional village in an English back-water, grabbed his attention completely. Five evenings a week, at quarter-to-seven, he'd tune in, and for those precious fifteen minutes the country folk of Ambridge would become part of his life.

On Saturday evenings it was horse racing. Then on Sunday afternoons I think it was a choice between the B.B.C. offerings of 'The Clitheroe Kid' or the 'Navy Lark' against the home produced 'School around the Corner,' presented by Paddy Crosby. I can still see the tears of laughter on his cheeks as he listened to the juvenile antics of Jimmy Clitheroe and later he'd be re-telling the funny story some child had related to Paddy Crosby.

On Wednesday nights, my mother did a night class. I was left up to listen to 'Gunsmoke,' the wild west adventures of Marshal Matt Dillon. 'Don't tell your mother,' he'd say, as he done my homework.

The absolute highlight of his week was any Sunday a hurling game was broadcast on the radio. The teams on the field were incidental, it was the game that mattered. Once the ball was thrown in and the commentary of Michael O'Hehir filled our kitchen with excitement. It also lifted our hopes and expectations.

My father would be held spellbound for the duration of the game. We'd listen together, facing each other, sitting on the old wooden kitchen chairs, knees almost touching, but minds locked together on the field of play, possibly more than a hundred miles away. If Cork were playing and Christy Ring put a goal in the opponents net; in the first few seconds as he often did, so much the better. The Railway Cup, the Munster Final and the ultimate game in Croke Park on the first Sunday in September. He listened to them all.

My father had originally come from a farming background, before the advent of diesel when horsepower was still in vogue. He was never a person blessed with luck; his clouds had no silver linings and nothing in life came easy.

Life was an endurance.

When I reflect, on what I remember, of the hardships of his everyday life, I've often wondered how he managed to keep his sanity. It can never have been easy, but he'd shrug his shoulders and carry on. The one thing he'd never do was quit.

In the church one time I heard a priest say,

'God loves most the one that tries.'

How did he know? I might have been naïve enough back then to believe it, but not anymore. I haven't believed it for a long time. No one could have tried harder than my father. He tried and tried and tried.

There is no other explanation for it, I think it must have been his faith. He's the only man I've ever known that had an unshakeable belief in God. An eternal optimist, he was always hoping for a brighter tomorrow, but unfortunately for him, that day never arrived.

An old black, single speed bicycle was forever his only mode of transport. My mother often referred to it as, *'The gadget with more squeaks than spokes.'* He pedalled the roads of East Cork on that bike, looking for work. Knocking on doors, that mainly remained unanswered.

Some days, a chink in the clouds, might let a little light shine through. He might get a week or two at haymaking, harvesting, or picking potatoes. Menial work, never much of it, and nothing that ever paid very much. If the weather turned wet, the work dried up. Once rain crested the horizon, the outcome was inevitable. They would find my father.

– 208 –

It is often referred to as the 'Hungry Fifties.' That was the decade he was often without work for long periods of time. Those were the years that people deserted this country by the boatload. The 'Innisfallen' steamed from the Cork quays a few times a week. It would be loaded to the gunnels with a cargo of humanity ready to feed the avaricious hunger of the burgeoning English labour market.

Those left behind waited on the letters. The scrawled lines describing life in another country never had quite the same importance as the Sterling notes tucked between the tear smudged pages.

It was from those letters that we learned of McAlpine, Laing, Murphys and the Titans of construction. Henry Ford, the man who made cars of every colour as long as they were black, hoisted the flag for manufacturing over Dagenham, and wasn't he from Cork, no less. No doubt, some succeeded and prospered; most did not.

My father hadn't the hands of a craftsman. I very much doubt that he could drive a nail straight.My mother never waited anxiously for a letter bearing the Queen's head on the stamp and a British postmark. My father; no longer a young man, didn't go.

He really had no need to go. He'd already been there and done that. In nineteen forty-eight he'd sailed half a world away, to Brazil in South America. Ninty per cent of those that sailed to Fishguard or Holyhead would never even have heard of it.

As soon as he'd settled, my mother (pregnant with me) was to follow, but she couldn't face the sea journey, which at that time was anything from six to eight weeks.

Somewhere in the vicinity of Sao Paulo, he worked at

managing a stud farm for Lord Something or Other, one of the British gentry that had large estates in that part of the world.

He came back from Brazil. Always a very quiet man, one of very few words, he was never one to boast of what must have been the adventure of a lifetime.

I had a question from school. Piranah fish, did he know anything about them? He did. It was one of the few times I recall him talking to me about Brazil. His words though are as fresh today as when he spoke them.

He'd been out riding early one morning, giving a young stallion some exercise before the day got too hot. The horse trod on something. The hoof was bleeding, the animal was lame. On the route back to the stable yard, he'd to cross a shallow river, about knee high at the crossing. In the space of a heartbeat the water appeared to boil. The horse was pulled down and literally torn apart. He told me he was lucky to reach the river bank and escape with no more damage than the bite marks on his boot heels. It was a story to stir the imagination of any child. I have no doubt it was true, my father would rather die than lie. It was the way he was.

Horses were his life's blood. Those magnificent equine animals were his forté. As Nijinsky could dance, or Hayden compose music, so could my father manage horses. More than that, he could understand them.

We were, I suppose a bit different to most people living on a council estate. Whereas other people kept a dog or a cat, our garden shed was converted to a stable and we always had a horse.

My father had been brought up with them. The horse wasn't born that he couldn't gentle. Race horses, hunting hacks and show ponies, their speciality didn't matter; he was the man to bring out the best in them.

Though he was respected far and wide for his knowledge of horses, not always was his talent, decency and downright hard work, repaid as it should have been. His good nature was more often than not badly abused by those he'd helped. People who should have treated him better.

However a horrendous fall at a race meeting in Dungarvan left him a broken shell of the man he'd once been, and almost brought about his demise. In a coma for over six months, he survived, but only just. It was probably a catalyst for later health issues.

It annoys me now to realise that I know so little about his life, in that I know absolutely nothing about his parents, as he never once mentioned them.

If one attempts something often enough the desired results will eventually come to fruition. Things did change, but only marginally for the better. He found employment on various long-term jobs. None of them great, but they paid the rent and put food on the table.

We drifted apart. I was searching for mythical heroes and looking for a life. I suppose it's what we do. I was so wrapped up in my own world to realise that his was slipping away.

The first time I took the boat to England at the end of the sixties, there were tears in his eyes as he shook my hand and pushed a ten-shilling note into my pocket. It was the end of an era.

I didn't smell the aroma of roses as I walked up the garden path. My father had been hospitalised for three weeks with heart problems, and I knew his condition was critical. I could see my mother inside the kitchen window, surrounded by neighbours. She was crying. I knew then that my father had passed away. I had visited him the previous day, never thinking it would be the last time for both of us.

My father died on the 17th of May 1972.

Thirty-seven years later, long after my search for a hero was forgotten, my eyes opened. In an old tattered 6x4 black and white photograph, hanging on the kitchen wall, I saw him for the first time. I shed tears that morning. I cried for the lost years and the words that were never spoken.

It took me sixty years to grow up. That long to realise what a fool I'd been. I hadn't needed to look for heroes; the one I had was bigger and better than any.

I'm sorry Dad. Not just for being so blind, but that it took me so long to see.

The Story of Kathleen Smith

*The moonlight through the window glass
illuminated the pages...*

I picked up the book from the shelf in my small attic bedroom, lifting it to my face, breathing in the particular odour that an old leather-bound book cover has. I lovingly caressed what was now and always had been my most cherished possession. It was a book that brought back a lot of memories.

I was standing beneath the skylight window of my room, in our two up, two down redbrick terraced house in Portswood, Southampton. The moonlight through the window illuminated the pages as they turned beneath my fingers, a memory on every page.

As I browsed, the details of each chapter were still as clear in my mind as the day I first read them. I had lived my life using this book almost like a bible that had been written just for me alone. A personal guide, my mentor. It had served me well in the past and would continue to do so in the future. At last I closed it, knowing when I did so, that I was closing the door on a large a chapter of my past life, but the door to new beginnings was just opening.

I wrapped the book in tissue paper, packing it away carefully in the bottom of my bag with some other personal items. The things I treasured that I would always keep with me. I picked up my bag and closed the bedroom door quietly. I didn't look back. My old life was over, the time had come to move on.

It was my last day in this house and my mind was flooded with memories. Some good, bad, sad, indifferent, all of them important.

I remembered clearly the very moment that book had been presented to me, looking back, it seemed like a lifetime ago, perhaps it was.

I would never forget that mid-December day in Ms. Buckmaster's Academy for Young Ladies. How proud I was, to stand there in the large assembly hall with the rest of the girls. When my name was called, I took, what I believed to be the longest walk of my life. With my head bowed, blushing furiously, I just prayed I was going in the right direction. The podium seemed miles away and the walk to take an eternity. As Ms. Buckmaster placed the book in my trembling hands. The other girls clapped and cheered good-naturedly. Tears of joy coursed down my cheeks. My heart thumped so much I thought I'd faint, if I didn't die first.

The book, a much-coveted special prize, was awarded every Christmas to the student who had conducted herself in an exemplary fashion and had made excellent progress. Ms. Buckmaster made a short speech as she congratulated me. I dabbed the tears from my eyes as my heart soared to the heavens.

I, Kathleen Smith, the only daughter of a settled traveller, had just received the very first brand new possession I'd ever been given in my short twelve years of life. It was a few days before Christmas 1896, the end of the school term, and my happiest moment ever.

After the presentation Ms. Buckmaster and the other school tutors held a surprise Christmas party for us. Each of us got a large glass of homemade lemonade, some sliced cake and biscuits.

When the party finished Ms. Buckmaster wished us all a very Happy Christmas and New Year, and a safe journey home for the holidays. I wrapped the book carefully in my long school scarf and clutched it tightly under my coat.

The winter chill blew in from the south-west, across the Isle of Wight, whipping the deep forbidding waters of the Solent into a white foaming frenzy. It was cold enough to hold the promise of a White Christmas. But I was beyond feeling cold, the warmth of pure joy coursed in a blood rush through my veins. I ran in the direction of home until I thought my legs would give out and I struggled to catch my breath. I passed the hustle and bustle of the Mary St. market. I ran by the second- hand clothes stalls, the meat vendor's counters, and the overpowering smell from the fishmongers.

On that day nothing mattered. I was oblivious to all. At the top of Mary St. I crossed the Northam Rd, dodging between the slow-moving carter's drays, and the quicker moving carriages of the gentry. My breath was coming in gasps, turning to white vapour as it hit the icy cold air.

In my twelve-year old mind, I was on cloud nine. This was the biggest thing that had ever happened to me, and up there was a star in the making. Kathleen Smith was a girl of some importance.

At last I reached home. Our house stood in a short cul-de-sac of red-bricked, back-to-back terraced houses in the Portswood area. I let myself in to our small yard through the narrow wooden gate. I found the big, iron backdoor key in its usual hiding place, under the geranium pot on the windowsill. I moved carefully, keeping as silent as possible. I didn't want to disturb my dad, whom I knew at this time of day would be dozing in his old chair by the empty fire grate.

My dad, Jethro Smith had been born the second son of an itinerant travelling family, from what's known as The West Country. I had never been to his home place, much and all as I'd have liked to go. In his early years, he'd worked as a horse-trader, scrap-metal dealer, rag and bone man, anyway he could turn a shilling or earn a pound. He'd picked hops in Kent, potatoes in Scotland. He harvested grain on the Isle of Wight, broke stone for the roads, and painted hay-barns in the summertime. He was a jack-of-all-trades, always on the move. A big, strong, dark skinned man of striking appearance. He always wore a red bandana around his neck and a small gold ring in his right ear. He always joked that the ring would provide the money for his funeral. His once, coal black hair was now showing a sheen of silver, as was the stubble on his cheeks.

Fourteen years he'd been married to my mother, a settled woman from Dorset. The union was frowned upon by the great majority of my mother's people, who took umbrage with what they saw as marrying beneath her. I was born soon after.

He gave up his life on the road for the sake of my mother and myself and got full-time employment on the docks of Southampton.

Then came the near fatal accident that left him so badly broken, he would never work again. This once powerful, able-bodied man was reduced to a shambling wreck. He'd been a loving husband and a good provider. A faithful and honest man. Though crippled, he never lost his dignity, or the light of pride in his dark brown eyes. Jethro Smith was more to me than a father; he was my best friend.

I entered the sitting room quietly and saw the old worn blanket covering his knees had slipped to the floor. It lay in a heap at his feet. I replaced it as gently as possible, tucking it in around him to ward off the cold. We couldn't afford to light the fire in the parlour before nightfall. Then the bright cheery blaze of the fire, in the gleaming black grate, added warmth as well as light to the neat and tidy room. The main light was provided by the two wax candles my mother bought weekly from old Mr. Isaacs shop on the corner of our road.

I set about preparing our evening meal and at four o'clock I lit the fire in the small cooking range in the kitchen. Then I filled the big, black cast-iron kettle from the tap in the yard. The sky was now black with an occasional snowflake drifting and dancing in the freezing air. I put the kettle on thinking of how my mam would enjoy a hot cup of sweet tea when she got in from work.

My mam worked in one of the larger houses in the upmarket area of the city. Her employer, a middle-aged gentleman, was a merchant banker and was also involved in something to do with the shipping trade. She worked six days a week, with Sundays off. She considered herself lucky to have employment at all; so many misfortunate people were dependant on the soup kitchens and bread lines. At least her employer treated her with a degree of respect and civility, not normally afforded to the working classes. Sometimes she got pieces of good quality material, from the family dressmaker, out of which she made my clothes. She also got to take home the remnants of their meals, and as they ate well, so did we. On Sundays, on what should have been her day off, she took in washing for people. Since my dad's accident, my mam had to do the best she could.

I had gone to the big house with her on Saturdays for a long time. I think maybe since I was about eight or nine. The old lady that lived there, the mother of my mam's employer had taken a shine to me. She used to get me to sit and read to her all day long. In summer in the gazebo house in the beautiful gardens. In winter in the well-appointed library in front of a huge log fire. She was a very kindly old soul and instilled in me a great love of books and reading.

My dad couldn't read, but that never made me think any the less of him. He was very happy for me to get an education, something that he'd never had himself.

It was the old lady, who with the consent my parents, arranged a scholarship for me. I was to receive a full education at *Ms. Buckmaster's Academy for Young Ladies.* At that time the foremost private school for girls, in Hampshire.

My mam came home from work. My dad woke from his slumber. We sat around the kitchen table and had our evening meal. Enjoying the cosy warmth of the heat from the range, the top now glowing red as the steaming kettle whistled and sang. Just as if it was heralding the arrival of good news. It was nice there in the kitchen, just talking and happy in each other's company. I cleared away the dishes and wiped clean the tablecloth.

My hands were shaking again as I put my prize, still wrapped in my school scarf on the table. Smiling to myself,

I opened it slowly, trying to keep my parents in suspense for as long as possible. Finally unveiling my prize, more precious to me than any jewel. My parents looked at it, not sure of what to say or what it meant. I explained.

My mam reacted first. 'On my word Jethro, will you look and see what our Kath has won?'

My dad was so overcome he cried with delight. I had never seen him so happy. The tears welled from his eyes, glistened on the silver stubble of his cheeks, as they trickled slowly to his chin. My mam just hugged me so hard I thought I'd break. Squeezing me so tight against her, all the while telling me how proud she was of me. She couldn't wait to get to work next morning to give the old lady the good news. It really was a never-to-be-forgotten day.

I didn't expect a Christmas present. My parents couldn't afford to waste the little money we had on luxuries. I didn't mind. On Christmas morning my mother surprised me with a beautiful new dress she had made me, and I had my prize, a book to cherish and keep with me always.

I read only a few pages a night in my small attic bedroom, the flickering light of the candle casting shadows all over the walls. Reading it quickly was out of the question. This book was so special, I had to make it last.

I spent three more years in the Academy, after I won that prize. It must have brought me a lot of luck; for after that my academic pathway was so smooth, it seemed strewn with rose-petals.

At the end of my last term there I won a scholarship, this time on my own merits, to train as a nurse at a top London teaching hospital. The view held by my parent's was that if the opportunity ever arose, I should avail of it. They wished me well for the future whatever the outcome would be.

I pursued my studies diligently in London: and my time there passed a lot more quickly than I would have thought possible. I resolved that when my training finished, I would return to Hampshire to be near my parents. They had provided for and supported me all my life; and now that they were getting on in years maybe it was time to try and pay something back. I secured a position in Southampton General and settled into the routine there. Though I lived in at the hospital; I was able to get home for a visit in my free time.

Then my dad passed away after a long illness. He bore the pain leading to his sad demise stoically. I never once heard him complain. My mam had given up work a few years previously to care for him and she took his passing very hard, but his loss left me devastated.

I don't know how word spread, but my dad's people came from all over for the funeral. Some of them came hundreds of miles. Not one of my mother's folk attended. I know this cut her to the quick and hurt her very deeply.

We discussed what we thought the future might hold for us. Too many long nights sewing by the candlelight had taken its toll of mam's eyesight. in whatever time she had left. I wanted to give her the best life I possibly could.

I had a little money saved, and with what we thought we might get for the sale of the house, we knew that we should be able to relocate to somewhere else without too much difficulty. I had seen an advert in a hospital newsletter for qualified nurses to take up posts in America. Plenty of opportunities available to suitable candidates. I made some enquiries and was accepted for an interview. These were held in a very upmarket hotel in Park Lane, London, and I travelled up by train to attend. Ten days later I received a letter offering me a contract. Suitable accommodation, in an apartment in close proximity to the hospital, would be secured for my mother and myself.

'Oh! The excitement of it all'.

We put the house on the market. As it was in a good location it sold quickly, and for a good bit more than we expected. We didn't want to live there anymore, too many memories, now that my dad had passed on.

We did then something that for us was completely out of character. We went on a shopping spree. We travelled into the city centre where all the big stores were and spent the length of a long day indulging ourselves. After the heartache and sorrow of the previous few months it was wonderful to hear my mother laugh again, and to see her spirits lifting, for the first time in months.

I had been advised that New York could be cold, so we bought some good quality clothing to cover every eventuality. To round off the day I treated my mam to a real slap up meal in a city centre hotel. It felt so good to be able to do so, just to be able to repay her in some small way for all the love and kindness she had always shown me. The following morning, we went to the offices of the White Star Line and booked our passage to New York for early April.

As the time drew near our apprehension mounted. Were we doing the right thing? What if we didn't like it? Would we ever see England again? So many unanswered questions, but it was the chance of a lifetime, wasn't it? For both of us a new start, a new life, in the New World.

*

I'll never forget what was to be our last morning in England. The 10ᵗʰ of April 1912. Closing the door behind us for the last time. Walking away from a house that held so many memories. A horse drawn Hansom cab was waiting to take us to the docks and despite the early hour a few neighbours gathered to wish us well. At the end of our road I looked back for one last time. My heart skipped a beat and a cold shiver ran through me. Perched on one of our front gate piers was a magpie.

We stood on Southampton docks as a cold chilling mist rolled in over the Solent. The whole atmosphere, and the early morning activity of dockland life was new to both of us, and we found it very exciting. The noise and clatter of steam derricks, cargo being loaded, orders being shouted. Dockers scurrying back and forth, coupled with the ceaseless babble of excited chatter from the waiting passengers. I overheard someone say that 914 passengers were embarking, and I couldn't believe that so many people could possibly be in one place. The tearful goodbyes on every street corner. The promises to write. Dreams and hopes an hour away from fulfilment. Dangling in the frost laden air, better things were now only just out of reach.

At nine o'clock the gangway was lowered, and a man dressed in a uniform, told us through a loud hailer that the ship would sail on the high tide at noon.

I clutched the frail hand of my mother, now damp with perspiration, despite the chill of the morning. I could feel her shiver, nervous with the anticipation of the unexpected. We moved forward slowly, as the previously loud chatter dropped to a low hum. Somewhere behind me a child began to cry. This was it, no going back.

My mother hesitated for a moment, then stepped on to the gangway. She glanced back and smiled at me reassuringly.

The bulk of the ship loomed over us. My heart filled with a new hope. Just then the image of that magpie, looking so ominous, crossed my mind. My dad, a mine of information on gypsy folklore, always said that one lone magpie spelt bad luck.

Well too late for that now. I offered up a silent prayer and clutching the back of my mother's coat, I gazed up at the great black bows of the Titanic.

Hey! Did Ye Hear
I was Robbed by a Guard?

I learned the hardest lesson of my life that day

I can recall that day now as if it was yesterday. Not the most pleasant of days to remember, I've had better, but certainly one I shall never forget. Looking back on it now, over half-a-century later, the incident itself was nothing major, but for that time the amount of money involved was, by most people's standards, huge. The events of that day are forever etched in my memory.

I learned a hard lesson that day, Did it make me a dishonest person? I'm not saying it did, but it certainly made me a lot less trusting than perhaps a lad of my age should have been.

When I crawled out of bed on that August Bank Holiday, it looked like being a gloriously hot day. I'd hardly time to pull my trousers on and breakfast was for other people. That morning I hit the stairs running and why wouldn't I? If there was a cloud in the sky it wasn't dangling over my head. I was half-way through my holidays and I was a busy boy.

I was going to the city for the day. Ten minutes later, after getting the usual lectures from my mother *'Mind yourself, don't talk to strangers, and be careful crossing the road,'* I was waiting for the bus to trundle through from Youghal. Oh yeah! Cork city, here I come.

In those days Cork was a safe place to stroll about of an afternoon. Sadly, those days are long gone. Back then I had a routine. I'd get off the bus at the terminal in Parnell Place and walk up Merchant's Quay, to Patrick St. Just by the statue of Father Matthew, (once the scourge of the Cork city drinkers) was a phone box.

My grandparents lived in the suburbs. I'd visit them most weekends. I'd do a few odd jobs. Split some firewood and collect eggs etc. for my grandmother and spend an hour or two reading for my grandfather, a man who'd never learned to read. I've no idea where he got it from, but I only ever remember him wanting the one book read to him. The pages were yellowed and the print miniscule and I must have read that book a hundred times.The covers were stiffened with cardboard and the whole thing held together with yards of various types of sticky tape. To this day it's still the same, though I've never opened it since he passed away.

Blissfully unaware that my action would trigger a chain of events that possibly defined the whole course of my future life, in I went to the phone box,

The phone was one of those ancient gadgets that by the time I was half-way through dialling, my finger was swollen and I'd forgotten the last few digits. Pressing button B to get the money back was a long standing joke. That damn button never returned a copper coin to anyone.

After a struggle with the cutting edge technology of the sixties I heard my grandmother on the line. 'Hello, hello, is that you?' 'Yes Nan, I'll be out in about half-an-hour.'

'Half-an-hour? What's going to delay you? Call to Ms. Finn and get me a packet of Fox's glaciers and Riche's Milky mints. Oh! Bring a few strawberry and blackcurrant jam tarts as well. Mind you don't drop them crossing that road.'

Call over, I looked about me. On the floor of the box was a lady's small handbag. I picked it up, looked inside, and the world as I knew it, imploded.

A woman's bag. If even seen in close proximity to such a piece of equipment I'd surely be ridiculed forever. Without appearing to do so, I looked about carefully. Eyes left, eyes right. I risked another peep inside. Blinked. Chanced another look and nearly passed out. To my eyes, the bag was crammed with more money than a Vatican vault.

Keeping my back to the door, I tucked it inside my shirt and under a arm. Looking like all the cares of the world belonged to someone else, I sidled out of the box. Within a minute I'd completed a sort of side-slip shuffle to the toilets on the quayside.

Dubiously safe in a cubicle, I tried not to breath too deeply as I emptied the contents of the bag on to the top of the cistern. Not much. A tube of bright red lipstick and a small comb. Mind you, it also contained the jackpot- nine hundred and four single pound notes. I know this because it took me at least half-a-dozen attempts to count them. I'd be almost there when I'd lose track. Was that five hundred and eighty or eight hundred and five? When I got the same answer twice I gave up.

Next move. I ran out of there faster than a world class sprinter after a red hot vindaloo. I stopped maybe three times to see if I was being tailed. The coast appeared to be clear. No one was screeching 'Stop Thief.' Though I've no doubt there was a woman, somewhere not too far away, rattled as a sack of angry wasps.

A plan is a handy thing to have. I tried to make one. Not the greatest idea I've ever had. My best one was 'Eenny, meeny, miney, moe, what shall I do with all this dough?'

Then I saw what I thought might be the answer. Horns honked and blew as I weaved my way through the traffic. I crossed the street and stood on the footpath for a minute, hoping for an extra shot of courage. Nothing doing, so no other option only go ahead with the plan. I entered the Garda Barracks.

Things were quiet. No activity. As if it was an every day event I sauntered to the desk. Ding-ding. No answer on the bell. I tried again. Harder this time. Ding-ding. Ding-a-ling-a-ling. Ding-ding-ding. Ding. Result.

'Alright, alright. What's all that bloody ringing about?'

I hadn't seen him at first. Up from behind the desk appeared a sleepy looking individual I took to be a guard. Well he was wearing the uniform. He scratched his head, yawned and rubbed sleep from his eyes. Then gave himself a scratch under the arms. We made eye contact...Eventually.

'Hmmmmmm! What can I do for you, young fella?'

I explained my predicament.I could see that most of my dilemna was falling on deaf ears. At the mention of money, he perked up. When he heard the amount, I had his interest.

A book was produced, one of those big old fashioned ledgers. Guard Sleepy suddenly became Guard Active. Dutifully he entered all the details.This involved a bit of pen-chewing and ear-scratching. Then he started counting the roll of readies.

'This is just procedure, you understand. Just to make sure it's all there.'

I was thinking it was going to take forever. It very nearly did. A few times he wiped sweat from his forehead, but after a count, and five or six recounts he pronounced him-self well satisfied. The final count, Nine hundred and four pounds.

'Well that's our business done young fella. Run along now and if it's not claimed in a year and a day it'll be all yours. G'wan! Off with ye.'

Was it a trick of the light or was he smirking?

Over the next fifteen months it gradually slipped from my mind, and I totally forgot about it. Hard to believe, but true. Passing the barracks one day, I made an enquiry.

'We'll have to get back to you.'

I had just reached home when a patrol car from the city stopped outside our house. My father, a God-fearing man, nearly had the mother of all strokes. The detective assured him. I hadn't done anything wrong, I was just assisting them with enquiries.

Within half-an-hour I was on the top floor of the bar-racks. In front of a panel of three plain clothes men. I was grilled. Everything was questioned. Did the bag really exist? Was the money a figment of my imagination? Had I made the whole story up? Their whole approach was of the *softly, softly, catchee, monkee* kind. No raised voices. Then came the sting in the tail.

There was no lady's bag containing nine hundrd and four pounds handed into Lost Property on the date in question or any of the adjacent dates of the previous year. I knew the time had been August Bank Holiday Monday at three o'clock. There was no record in the book for that time or date.

It beggared belief. The money had gone. Vanished with-out trace. I had been robbed by a guard.

The Officer

The only sound was of the man's breathing...

The sweat formed in beads, then trickled slowly down the forehead of the man. The small airless room was hot, oppressive and uncomfortably humid. The sweat ran in rivulets through the stubble of his cheeks, down the bridge of his nose, to form a large droplet, which dangled precariously from the end, for a few seconds before splashing onto the tabletop. It formed in pools under his armpits, adding to his discomfort. Not even the ticking of a clock intruded on the stillness. The only sound was of the man's breathing.

The man looked around slowly. Taking in his surroundings, but without really seeing anything. Soon he knew the interrogation would begin. Hardly blinking, he watched as the droplets of sweat reflected the light from the single fluorescent tube hanging from the fly-blown ceiling. A large cobweb, the corpse of a long dead blue-bottle still entangled in the ragged looking web, dangled from a corner near the door.

The room was sparsly furnished, in that it contained a grey, metal filing cabinet, a long narrow wooden table and two mis-matched chairs. One, where the man sat, was high-backed, uncomfortable and made from some type of unyielding hardwood. The armrests were worn smooth from the occupancy of previous victims, over the passage of countless years.

The other chair was a padded, black swivel of the type most commonly used in offices. It was vacant now, waiting on the arrival of the interrogation officer. On the otherwise bare table-top was a telephone of a non-descript colour. A cheap calendar, the type that shows every day of the year, on a single sheet, was pinned slightly askew, to the back of the graffiti covered plywood door. The single tack, in the center near the bottom, caused the outer corners to curl upwards.

Faint at first, but growing louder, footsteps sounded from the corridor. The door opened silently. The interrogation officer stared silently for a long moment. The man still sat with head bowed. Waiting. No words spoken. A fly buzzed through the still open door. The man never moved as it perched on his sweat soaked forhead.

The officer entered and closed the door quietly behind him. He skimmed through a thin sheaf of papers he held in his left hand. Seemingly satisfied, he pulled out the swivel chair and sat down. There was no word of greeting offered. Nothing, that might have disturbed the cloying silence.

He was a tall, slightly built, bespectacled man. His thinning hair was combed across the top of his head to camoflage his baldness. He wore a shapeless, dark grey suit, shiny from wear at the elbows and the knees. A white shirt and a blue tie, washed once too often, completed his attire. A few inches below the knot, a soup stain, like a mono-chromatic motif decorated his tie.

The officer stared at the man on the opposite side of the table for a long minute. It seemed to be for eternity. His voice, when he finally spoke, was in a dull, monotonous drone. Uninteresting, almost accentless. The voice was as colourless as the man. It was the voice of a person, people lived near all their lives, but never saw, never remembered.

Then the interrogation began. The first questions came easy. The usual stuff. Name, address, date-of-birth, national insurance etc.

The man had been briefed over the previous week by the best in the business. Experts all. People who knew the score. Some had been veterans of long and ardous campaignes. Some were embroiled in skirmishes on a daily basis.

The man in the quiet corner of the bar. Anonoymous, face constantly hidden behind a news paper. He spoke only from the side of his mouth, the need for secrecy paramount. He was well experienced and been in this situation many times. A man to be heeded.

This morning, the woman on the bus who'd sat beside him. She'd never even looked at him, just spoke in a hushed whisper, for his ear's only. 'Concentrate, concentrate. Pick a spot on the wall. Keep your eyes focussed on that spot, nothing else matters. There is nothing else. Tell them nothing they don't already know. If you feel yourself weakening, and you think you should answer, be as economical with the truth as possible. Remember this is war. It's us and them, so the less they know the better for all concerned.'

When she got off at a stop before him, he realised, he didn't even know her name.

The voices in the man's head never switched off. The spot on the wall took his whole attention. It was true what he'd been told. He could see nothing else, because there was nothing else.

The officer shuffled the papers in front of him. One was selected seemingly at random. The never-ending questions continued relentlessly. On and on. The only sound now in the quietness of the room was the occasional scratching of the officers pen.

His concentration wavered. He knew he was close to breaking point. Without warning and to intense relief, the questions stopped.

The officer shuffled the papers into a neat pile, before replacing his pen in the breast pocket of his suit coat. He stood up. Putting both hands on the table, he leaned over and looked the man straight in the eye. Intimidating.

'You and I will, no doubt, meet again.' He said. *'You may go now, good day to you.'*

The man nodded his head. Tongue too swollen to venture a reply.

He staggered down the stairs and walked blindly out into the warm sunlight and the busy mid-morning bustle of the street. It felt friendly out here. A far cry from the interrogator's office.

Getting his breath back he walked rapidly for a hundred metres, dodging shopping bags and baby buggies, putting as much distance between himself and the office door as possible.

Then he stopped. Relaxing, if one could call it that, for the first time in what seemed an age. An empty bench by the park gate, beckoned to him. He sat, breathing in deeply, exhaling slowly.

Was this really the end or just the beginning? The things one has to endure to claim housing benefit.

I'm a Believer
(of sorts)

'**O**uch!' Where the f**k did that come from? One moment I'd felt on top of the world, the very next second, I was cursing the sudden affliction, that in less than a heartbeat was knocking seven sorts of stuffing out of me. Pain, worse than what I imagined a shark bite might inflict lanced like fire from my ankle to my knee. The pain was so bad I felt like screaming. Instead I gritted my teeth and tried to stay vertical, but that's a man thing. Don't show weakness.

It was 7am on a bright sunny morning and I'd just come off a night shift. I'd a six months lease on a flat in Kilkee. That was twelve miles away and how in the hell was I going to get there? I took a deep breath (actually it was a lot more than one) and dragged myself to my car. Putting my faith in the hands of whichever of the Gods was on duty, I squeezed myself behind the wheel and endeavoured to get home.

About 1.30 I woke from a pharmaceutical induced sleep. The pain was still bad and I gave serious consideration to sending the landlady out for a humane killer and ending the story.

No! Again, some vestige of foolish male pride grabbed the reins, and steered me away from going to see a doctor. A bit of pain wasn't going to beat me. I put my good leg on the floor. Fine. Tried the second leg. Sore but manageable. I could stand and limp after a fashion. I leaned on the window ledge and looked down on the beach. A beach that was at that time of the day shimmering like a jewel in the glorious September sunshine. That made my mind up.

The useless leg I dragged behind me, and hobbled towards those golden sands and a paddle in the blue Atlantic.

I'd a couple of hours to kill and decided to limp about a bit. The slope up the cliff path was gentle. The views were more than just a bit spectacular. I won't deny I'd spasms of real pain, but at that time I was basically fairly fit. A bit of discomfort wasn't going to stop me.

At the top I spent some time marvelling at what I could see of the West Clare coastline. That vast expanse of sea was shot through with a myriad of blues and greens. The sun reflected off the rippling wavetops. Here and there, calm pools reflected the few lazily drifting clouds. Breathing that clean air with the tang of salt on it was, for the moment in it, quite wonderful.

Across the road some sheep were grazing the verges.

'Hello,' I wondered aloud. 'What's that all about?' I crossed to the other side for a better look. On a whitewashed stone pillar letters crudely painted in black, proclaimed that this was the well of St. Chaoide. Not a saint I was familiar with. I'd never heard of him before.

Standing in the centre of a small meadow about thirty yards distant, and built like a tiny church, the well had been whitewashed until it gleamed.

Curiosity got the better of me. I dragged myself through the narrow gap in the old stone wall, and that's where my story begins.

I staggered across the meadow to the edge of the well. Not much to see really, just a pool about two feet across. A sliver of sunlight filtered in and caused the water to shine like mirror glass.

In for a penny...I pulled the boot off my aching leg and plunged it into the ice-cold water.

Bumble bees buzzed, flitting about the brambles. I heard something rummaging through the vegetation behind me. A curious old Polly had wandered through a hole in the ditch to see what the intrusion was about. A hoard of midges hovered about her. The discerning bovine snorted disdainfully. I was of no interest. Then with a flick of her tail, she departed, taking the fly family with her.

A quarter of an hour later, I extracted my well chilled leg from the water. I lay on the grass to dry off and that's when my day took a peculiarly interesting development.

I can truthfully swear to the second I draw my final breath, that the sensation I felt was unbelievable. Like water being poured from a bottle, the pain drained completely from my aching limb.

No! It didn't just vanish, it ebbed slowly from my knee, all the way to my toes. It shook me. I was totally dumbfounded, shell-shocked, call it what you will.

Was it miraculous? To me, it certainly was. I tried standing, walking, kicking, every move I could think of, all without a bother.

With the sun going down behind me I headed back to the village. This time I took the road and found I could jog if I felt like it. Thankful for small mercies, I didn't tempt fate. Besides it was time for dinner.

As well as renting me a flat, Mary Ryan, my landlady, also had a café and that woman could lay on some spread. I ate there every evening before work, and I was never less than well satisfied. The only problem was that she had a bit of an affliction that appears to be common to most women.

Inquisitiveness wasn't in it with her. She was one nosy woman. Every waking moment of my day she'd want to know about, and that lady had ways of making me talk. She pulled up a chair and began the nightly interrogation.

'Well,' says she. 'How did you get on today? Where did you go? What did you see? Did you meet anyone? You never came in for the breakfast this morning, was there something ailing you? Of course, it's no business of mine, but if I don't know these things, I'd be feeling I wasn't looking after you properly. Do you see what I mean? That's all right isn't it? Now! While you're getting that fine feed down you, be telling me where you went and what you saw. Leave nothing out.'

What choice did I have? I sang like a canary. She listened without a comment until I crossed the road to the well.

'What well would that have been?' She asked.

I explained. I told her everything there was to tell. Twice over and in great detail. Her son was at the next table. He was called over and I had to go through it again. Reinforcements were called up in the shape of the cook from the kitchen. A couple of women waiting on the weekly bingo bus were also recruited. I was getting nervous. Heads were shaking. There was doubt etched on every face. It was clear that Mrs. Ryan didn't believe a word of it.

The Clare woman thought very deeply for a minute before giving her verdict.

'No son. It couldn't have happened like that. Your leg could not have been cured above at that well. Wherever else it happened, it wasn't there.'

'I think it was,' says I. 'Sure where else was I?'

She patted my hand as if I was an errant child. 'No! God love you son, there's no blame on you, but being from Cork ye weren't to know that there are two wells. That one you called to is the well for the eyes. St. Chaoide is better than an optician. He's a great man for the eyes altogether. The well for the legs is a few miles away, in the opposite direction.

I was gobsmacked. Should I laugh or cry. The Clare woman grabbed her coat and led the charge to the bingo bus.

Jack, Shine on You Crazy Diamond
In Memory of a Great Friend

Not a place I would have chosen for a reunion but when things happen that way who amongst us can say they are not meant? **I** stood at the door of the hospital room in C.U.H. for maybe a minute wondering which of the beds I was searching for. Only one had the curtain pulled around, shielding the occupant from view. The curtain swished back. The nurse emerged and the man in the bed turned his eyes in my direction. Like a light switch being thrown the eyes behind the spectacles shone in recognition. His whole face lit up.

'Olly?' More of a question then a statement, the first word I'd heard spoken by him in almost thirty years. He struggled to sit more upright; but couldn't. He was just as I remembered. The light in the eyes behind the glasses shone just as bright as the last time I'd seen him. He was always slightly built so no change there. His once luxuriant red hair was still lengthy, but a lot thinner, other than that it was certainly the same Jack O'Regan.

A letter had been delivered to me the previous weekend by a former patient that had been in the adjacent bed. It was letter that rolled back a lot of years.

From the mid-seventies I didn't have much contact with the city and subsequently lost touch with the few friends I had there. The letter asked could I go and see him, not a problem. I was working away somewhere at the time but could get to the city the following weekend.

That visit was the renewal of a great friendship, the time span of which unfortunately was all too brief.

We chatted for perhaps an hour that day. All the usual things people speak of that haven't met for years. Do you remember...? Did you see...? I wonder what happened to...? Wasn't it sad about...? We solved the problems of the nation until the bell rang, and the visiting hour was up.

In the space of a brief hour on a Saturday afternoon we were attempting to catch up on the events of half a lifetime. His eyes were closing; his sister explained that he got tired easily, but he'd been looking forward to the visit all week and would I call again. Of course I would. I left my phone numbers and promised to repeat the visit on the following week. I gripped his hand to say goodbye but his head was on his chest and Jack O'Regan was asleep.

How the course of people's lives diverge! One day your there and the next through some simple twist of faith the pathways of friends are never crossed again.

Late the following week I got a call that surprised me, it was from Jack to say he was at home in Glasheen. I'd be welcome to call anytime. I was well pleased to hear he'd been discharged from hospital and as that same week I was changing jobs, I called on the Tuesday night.

He re-introduced me to his brother Joe; another face that took me back years. Back to the steps of what used to be the Savoy cinema, where on a Saturday afternoon you were guaranteed to meet just about anybody. Doing Pana as it was called at the time.

Jack would always be there at some time on a Saturday. Always with the Melody Maker folded under one arm, always with a smile on his face. A face that never frowned or wore the mask of bad humour. Always there seemed to be something good going on in his life, and his good-natured disposition rubbed off on those around him.

He was an encyclopaedia on all matters pertaining to music, both local and international and would share his knowledge with anyone.

He was the original pirate, being the first person in Cork to set up his own radio station, Radio Skywave and he was a brilliant sound engineer. He ran a blues club for a while near the old blood bank on Leitrim St. If someone had a query relating to music Jack O'Regan was the man to ask. He could always be seen filming the concerts in the City Hall, likewise the gigs at the Cavern Club on Leitrim St. later known as the 006.

All the time I knew him I never asked what his illness was. I must have been very naïve. It never occurred to me that people got sick and didn't recuperate. It was just something that never crossed my mind.

I visited with him as often as I could after that at the house in Glasheen. He lived with his mother, a lovely lady of the old school. No two people could ever make someone more welcome. Sometimes he'd call me and tell me not to come if he wasn't feeling well. Right up until the end I was blissfully unaware of just how seriously ill he was.

One night I got a call from Joe to say Jack was being shifted to Marymount. I thought that was some sort of a rest home for sick people until they recovered properly. I was quite pleased about it; I thought it would be good for him.

Marymount! A name that rolls easily off the tongue. A name that's easy to say. For me it conjured up an image of an old stately home and acres of well-tended gardens; perhaps a place where in bygone days, if the weather was warm, genteel ladies took tea on the lawn under the shelter of a parasol and indulge in a spot of croquet to while away a sunny afternoon.

The sort of place where gentlemen might enjoy a brandy and port while discussing affairs of state and the business of the day as the commercial life of the city unfolded below them undisturbed by the passage of the Lee to the lower harbour.

How wrong could I be? How could a name be so misleading? Until I visited Jack I had no idea that Marymount was a Hospice for the dying; the last refuge for those with very little left to look forward to, a place where death is mostly welcome and not governed by the dictates of the visitors bell.

Death can call at any time, and usually does. I'd like to think that the death that calls to Marymount is not the tall, gaunt, sickle wielding reaper of souls; that death has its own agenda for those that need it. After all the Grim Reaper never asks permission and has no use for door keys.

No! I think the Marymount death takes those in its care to a paradise that's free of pain, where good weather prevails, and angels (real ones) serve drinks in the bar to the background sounds of eternal happiness. For many people Marymount Hospice is the last stop on a line that (hopefully) leads to a better place, somewhere like I've just described. If such a place exists, I know that Jack O'Regan arrived there safely. He'd deserve no less.

I remember the last time I visited I brought him the Echo. I just threw it on the bed, as one does. I can still see the agony on his face and could almost feel the pain such an unthinking, innocuous act caused him. It was the last time I saw my friend Jack O'Regan alive.

I'll always be grateful that a place like Marymount exists. In a perfect world it might not be needed, but by being there it allowed a great friend and a very brave and gentle man to die as he had lived, with complete dignity.

I'll never forget Jack; he was the sort of person you'd walk on hot coals for and a gentleman to his fingertips. He was someone that faith dealt a cruel hand, but as was typical of the man he played that hand without complaining. It was just a game he couldn't win.

Jack became a patient of Marymount Hospice on Mayday. His family took him home to Glasheen for his 50th birthday on the 16th of that month; he went back the following day and died there on the 30th May 1998.

You were well loved my friend, and sorely missed.

Shine on, you crazy diamond.

Cute Hoors and Chancers

Those with an eye on the main chance.

The first one that comes to mind, (to protect the guilty), I'll call him 'D.' A really affable, good-humoured man, with an eye that was constantly on the main chance. He used to work, but no one, could ever recall him doing anything. Back in the seventies, the biggest construction site in the country was on the banks of the Shannon. To 'D' that site was like all his birthday presents had been delivered at once.

One day, crossing the site, he found a brief case. Inside, was an expense account book belonging to one of the management team. 'D' took it home and studied it. The company had ninety-day credit terms with a hotel in Ballybunion. That same evening he booked the wife and kids in there for three weeks holidays. Safe in the knowledge they'd be long gone before a bill was sent out.

On Derby day one year, he didn't go to work. In an early morning pub in Cork he got a tip he was assured couldn't lose. No money. What to do?

Every day on the way home the bus he used travel in stopped at a country pub for an hour. "Dennis" had a plan. He rang the land-lady and asked her to have a hundred on the nose for him. With the luck of the devil, the horse romped home at 9/1 Leaving him with a tidy pot of £1000. He stuck his thumb out and hitched it to North Cork.

I asked what he'd do if the horse lost. He shrugged his shoulders. 'It didn't though, did it.'

He was a story-teller par excellence, but he couldn't contain his talents. Everywhere he went, there was at least twelve to twenty men, standing about, laughing heartily, enthralled by his escapades. Eventually the company could take no more. The solution. *'Would you ever consider staying at home? We'll post your wages out every week, until the job is concluded.'*

A sweet deal, and he was up for it. It was like offering him two years paid holidays, but the unions objected. It just wasn't feasable. Every man should have the same entitlements.

The last time I saw him, I was sitting in my car in a cemetery. It was four o'clock on a Sunday afternoon. He was staggering through the churchyard on his way from the pub. I was afraid to make eye-contact. On previous occasions, I'd found it led to only one outcome. I'd go on my way, laughing, but a hell of a lot poorer.

He stopped. I watched. He checked the discarded flowers in the churchyard skip and made his selection, adding a few extra that were still usable. Then, beneath the tap, he freshened them up, shook the excess water off, and wobbled his way home.

I could see his house across the way. His wife, was in the garden. The man had style. I watched, in total fascination as with much aplomb and gallantry, the bouquet was presented. I have to admit, I was quite green at the reception he was given. The kissing and hugging seemed to go on forever. Then, the flowers were abandoned. She dragged him indoors. Romance blossomed, on that cold October evening.

The second gentleman I've called 'C' The tales about his exploits are legion. I've just included two. Gold Cup day at the Cheltenham Festival, sometime during the early sev-

enties. The chosen killing ground was in a lounge of the
Victoria Hotel in Cork city. The Horsey crowd had come
to town. All sheepskin coats, shiny shoes, and (most importantly), bulging wallets. Nobody paid any attention to the
the quiet man in the corner.

A card game started. Slowly at first, but within an hour,
the stakes were high and climbing. Someone scooped a large
pot. The quiet man had the measure of them. He started
taking an interest in the game. He knew the jargon of racing
men. Calling players by their names, in no time at all he'd
made himself familiar with them. He commiserated on los-
ing hands and gave encouragement to winners.

He was one of them. Every time a drink was called, he
was included. The big race started and finished. As the favourite obliged, amidst the clapping, cheering, foot-stamp-
ing and back-slapping, the quiet man sized up the odds. No
one paid him any heed. At five o'clock, he stood up, drained
his glass and produced a betting slip.

*Right lads, it's been great meeting up with ye, but I'm away to the
bookies to cash this little beauty. I'll only be about twenty minutes.
There's a long day there yet. We'll have a good drink when I get
back.*

Like stunned fish, he reeled them in. All around the table, winning dockets were produced and handed over.

*Here. As your at it collect mine. And mine. Hey, don't forget
about me.*

The soft-spoken, totally forgettable man departed. His
timing was perfect. The winning dockets were cashed. The
"Echo Boys" of Cork, scurried about the streets. The quiet
man legged it to the bus terminal.

At six-fifteen, he was on the bus home.

At just about that the same time, one of the horsey set, posed a question.

Hey John. Your friend is taking rather a long time. Any idea where he's got to?My friend? I thought he was with you.

In an upstairs lounge of the Victoria Hotel, mayhem was on the menu. Pandemonium broke out. '

Oh my God! We've been robbed. He was with you. He wasn't. He was with him so. I never saw him before in my life.What did he look like? How do I know? I'd me feckin' back to him. Should we call the guards? Are ye serious? And have me wife find out.'

It transpired that no one knew him, or had ever seen him before. No good filing a complaint. No one could remember what he looked like, or could hazard a guess at where he might have come from. The "Hooray Henrys" of the racing circles had been well and truly saddled. The quite man had slipped into their world and in the course of a couple of hours, had given them an evening to remember, or one, they'd never forget.

That was 'C.' As likeable a man as one could wish to meet, but boy, was he sharp. An opportunity wouldn't arise before he'd be on it.

Two of my friends, Mary and her sister Ann, were in the church yard. Mary was driving. She got her purse out and handed Ann, two twenty-pound notes.

All you have to do is go in there, find the Sacristan, and give him that money. Tell him I sent you. He knows what it's for.

Five minutes later, money delivered, Ann returned.

Has that Sacristan got a drink problem? No! Certainly not. Why

do you ask?
Well, he's in there now, so pissed he can hardly stand. The man is
wobbling all over the place.
No! No! No! You're mistaken.
I'm telling you he is. Go and see for yourself.
Ah no! I don't believe it.

Down the steps from the church door, staggered the
infamous 'C.' He held the two twenties to the light, and examined them, scarcely able to believe his luck.

He went in the church hoping for a miracle. He didn't
expect it that fast, and right inside the house of God. Shell-
shocked and fuming, Mary put the car in gear and drove
away.

Memories of my Mother
'Wash that bloody tide mark off your neck'

'*Get up for school. Wash your face, don't forget behind your ears and wash that bloody tide mark off your neck.*'

I think those the first words I ever remember my mother saying to me. They probably stuck because they were repeated almost every morning of my early years.

When I woke this morning, I had no clue as to what lay ahead. I never thought my mind would be cast back over seventy long years, to the day I started my first and most enduring love affair.

'G'wan,' I hear you say. 'What rubbish. How could that be?'

Well I'll tell you. I was born in a Cork City nursing home on the 08/12/1948. My mother was the first woman I ever saw. I didn't know what it was back then, but I do now. It was love and I fell into it. Seventy-one years later and I'm still loving her. My mother passed away on 02/12/2000.

As a woman she was strikingly good looking, and I've often thought that if the cards had fallen differently for her, what she could have made of herself, for she touched the lives of all who knew her.

Back then in the post-war years, life was tough. A good day was when it was a little less tougher than the previous day had been. It was an existence of scrimping, scraping and making do. That woman could adapt to any situation. Quite simply she was a great person, with a good heart. It's not easy looking back on it now, and I've no shame in saying it, but I've shed tears when I think of her. That woman, my mother, always had my back. She was the very best. The greatest single influence on my life, and until the day I'll die, I'll love her for it.

My mam (that's what I called her) was a very gifted individual and a free spirit. Years before in her younger days she'd been offered a scholarship to an art college in Scotland, but her parents wouldn't allow her attend. Pity; who knows what she might have achieved, because she really could turn her hand to anything. The woman had an amazingly strong work ethic, and if something needed doing, she'd find a way to do it.

An old knitting machine she acquired for making socks, was worked to full capacity during the winter months. Often she'd be working into the small hours. Those socks were much sought after by farmers and people doing heavy work. In summer when the agricultural shows were being held, she was much in demand for grooming and plaiting show ponies and horses.

She loved flowers and the garden in front of the house was a riot of colour all summer long.

When we'd come from school of an evening she'd be listening to Mrs. Dales Diary on the radio and usually baking something on the lines of scones, apple tarts etc. She was an excellent cook, and in September, twice a day, she'd be in the fields, mornings and evenings, picking mushrooms. She'd an uncanny knack of knowing the best places to go.

I couldn't ever say she was a woman with great religious leanings, but the one bit of advice she always gave me was to beware of those that proclaimed to be on God's right hand.

'Remember boy,' she'd say, *'The road to hell is paved with the souls of evil nuns and priests.'*

How right she was.

After my father passed away in 1972 life for my mam entered a different phase. She'd always been popular and made friends easily, but she became more outgoing, if that was possible. As the widow's allowance wasn't worth a damn, she decided to enter the work circuit. Probably not easy for someone who'd always been a stay at home wife, but she was nothing if not determined.

After a couple of seasons in the fish processing plant she'd started work in the canteen of a large meat company. She'd barely learned the run of the place, when suddenly one morning, the manager was dispensed with. Gone, let go, fired or whatever. No one left in charge. When tea-break time came around the workers (lots of them), were banging on the door and shouts of strike were being heard.

A man came down from head office. Get these workers fed, he'd ordered. Can't be done he was told, there's nobody in charge. The man was thinking on his feet or in a blind panic (no one knows for sure). Who wants the job? A lot of negative headshaking followed. My mam must have nodded. Okay, you have the job. Get 'em fed pronto, if they're happy, we'll draw up a contract.'

By lunchtime she was officially the new canteen manager. From rags to riches. Overnight she was making more money than she knew what to do with. Within a few weeks she'd purchased two massive mobile homes and berthed them across the road from Charles Fort near Kinsale, a really beautiful seaside location. The future was looking good.

For my mam, the mobile homes proved a worthwhile investment. She had one rented out continually and the other was for her own use. In no time at all, she was as well known around Kinsale and Summercove, as she was at home.

She met an Englishman that had settled there. An elderly gentleman whom she seemed to get along with. High on their list of social outings was always a trip to Liverpool for Grand National week.

This man had an artificial leg. One year they were queueing at the turn styles for entry when an unfortunate accident occurred. Weaving through the traffic came an impatient biker. He was the real deal. All chrome and black leather, with a backpatch on his jacket. He hit my mam's friend and blew his leg off. When he saw what had happened, the lights went out instantly and he hit the deck. The Bulldog Breed was reduced to Timothy Tabby. A quivering mass of pussycat.

My mam's friend (Rocky) was sitting on the kerb, trousers around his ankles, as he struggled to harness his leg back on again. Every time the biker boy surfaced for air, he took a look at the guy with one leg and promptly fainted again.

A year or two later Rocky was moving on, he'd sold his property and was retiring to live in Spain. Having a farewell drink in his local, on the day he was departing; tragedy struck. In the midst of the handshakes and goodbyes, a surprise ending. He dropped down dead.

My mam always did have an adventurous streak. If a bit of harmless fun was to be had, then she was up for it. She was very friendly with a single lady of about her own age that lived close-by.

This lady was what could only be described as flamboyant in the extreme. A lovely person. She was a real character and lived up to it. I think she might have been more suited to living decades earlier, as she always dressed and acted as star from the first days of film. She was extremely well read and could recite long passages of classical poetry without a bother.

Her hair and make-up were always perfect, as were her outfits, even though they were from a different era. She might have been caught in a time-warp, but she certainly lived to the style she'd created. This woman today, would most likely be termed a head-turner.

Having a drink one night, they'd met up with a young man from the Netherlands. He would best be described as a very naïve businessman, out to impress. In town for a few days, he was completely taken in by the aura of glamour exuded by my mam's companion.

Over the course of a few nights, he fell for her. Hopelessly in love or hook, line and sinker; take your pick, but this man was smitten. He, however, was going back to the Holland after a few days. Pedal to metal. The romance moved into overdrive.

'Marry me,' says Joshua. 'Indeed then I will,' says Phyllis. 'When?' says he. 'Well I'm not doing anything tomorrow.' says she.

Joshua was as good as his word. A week or so after his departure two tickets arrived for flights to Holland. One for the love of his life and the other for her Maid of Honour, my mam.

Off the pair of them went to the lowlands of Holland. Land of windmills and tulips. There the plans for the romance of the century quickly unravelled faster than a tumbleweed attacked by a tornado.

Apparently, Joshua (the poor innocent) forgot to mention that even though his family were mega billonaires, he himself hadn't a bean. His mother held the purse strings and that purse was tightly closed.

The man was sorely embarrassed when he introduced his soon-to-be-bride to the family matriarch. My mam told me after that it was only the luck of the Irish that the meeting was held behind closed doors. After the initial introduction, when his mother's temper hit the roof, and she went into total meltdown, Joshua wilted and agreed the whole thing was a mistake.

He went and cowered in a corner, as the tirade of abuse got ever louder. Though they had no clue as to what the lady was calling them, it was clear from her shrirking and gestulating that it was nothing complimentary. Poor old Joshua wasn't quite sure if he was being cut out of the will or she was having him beheaded.

She certainly made it clear that no son of her family was going to marry an Irish adventuress. They were left in no doubt that this lady was by no means a shrinking violet or indeed a tulip from Amsterdam.

With the wedding plans in tatters, they'd no option but to fall back on plan B. Accept defeat, return home, and live to fight another day. Another day arrived soon enough.

'...Ah mother, will you make your mind up? I know you'll love it. It'll be the adventure of a lifetime. It's all paid up. Don't back out now.'

The voice belonged to my sister Rita, having a bit of a job trying to persuade my mam to go on a safari to Africa. I think the mother was playing hard to get. More pressure was applied. 'G'wan you'll have a great time; you know you will.'

Rita had worked in Africa for some time so knew the lay of the land. She'd the safari booked. Everything was in order.

' Ah, but Rita…' 'Never mind the excuses.'

In the end there was only going to be one outcome. My mam was unashamedly a sunworshipper. On the chosen date, she was bound for Kenya, and loving it.

They were met by one of the tour guides. A tall, fit looking native, who towered above his two charges. 'Follow me please.' He set off as if he was taking it easy in a marathon. The pair he had in tow struggled to keep up. They were still in Nairobi airport when ma. gasped. 'Hey Rita,' No answer. She tried again, 'Hey Rita,' she wheezed. 'Jesus Almighty, would you slow down.'

'What? What's up now mother?' An out of breath Rita gasped in reply.

'Have you noticed this place is full of black people?'

They joined the rest of the group and in large 4X4s were soon heading for the outback. There were various camps along the route from which they could travel out daily to view an enormous variety of animals in their natural habitat. The place they were going to was called Treetops, which incidentally, had a moment of fame years before. It was there that a young Princess Elizabeth received the news of her father's demise. She had to return immediately to England to take over the throne. It was a beautiful spot, lots to see and gorgeous weather.

On the fourth evening, a fully grown male baboon wandered into the camp. The guides warned everyone to stay well back from him, as apparently this particular gentleman was anything but, and was well known to have a vicious streak.

Like the bad guys in Clint Eastwood westerns, this boy had an aura of danger about him. Oh yeah, he was a mean motherfucker. He looked like he meant business. Bad business. He was struttin' like he was waiting for a shootout. He got one.

Rita was busy taking photos. She'd left her rucksack on the ground. The tall, dark stranger was for having it. He picked the bag up, and all hell broke loose. The outlaw was challenged.

Faster than blinking, mam had him in a headlock. She'd no idea of the temper or strength of baboons. Bad Baboon hurled the bag into the trees and turned on her. He picked her up and threw her about twenty feet, before he pounced. She was lying dazed when he struck. She looked up and completely froze. All she could see was this huge open mouth, exposing fangs nearly three inches long. His mouth snapped shut, just at the same instant as one of the guides bent an iron post over his skull. Bad Baboon, distracted for an instant, missed his target, which was my mam's throat, and sunk those big yellow fangs into her upper arm. She passed out.

After getting thumped a few more times he backed off and swung himself back into the trees. A doctor was called. The bite was bad, she'd lost a lot of blood. There was a high risk of infection, possibly gangrene, which would be caused by whatever rotten food he'd clinging to his molars. One of the fangs touched the main arm bone between the elbow and the shoulder. She was confined to bed in a state of shock and confusion. When the medic was satisfied there was no risk of infection, he filled her with anti-biotics and discharged her.

For the rest of the trek, she was treated as a heroine. Everyone wanted their photo taken with her. The rest of the group had only seen the animals, she'd actually wrestled with one, which granted her special status. The story however was not over.

The guide gave them a warning. Keep the windows and doors locked at all times. He said the baboon now had mam's scent and would want to finish the job. Mam was hanging on every word, but Rita took all this with a grain of salt. Thinking it was just stuff for the tourists. Something to add an element of danger to the African experience. It wasn't.

During the midnight hours there was a banging at the window. They lay there petrified at first, then decided to investigate. When the curtains were pulled back the snarling face of Bad Baboon was about two inches away on the other side of the glass. Those big yellow fangs were ready for business. Luckily for them the windows were barred.

Rita had a theory that the old boy was looking for a mate and he'd decided a fine wrestler like my mother would fit the bill nicely. From then on, every night when they were in residence, he took up position outside the window. Mam found it a bit nervy, staring at those blood shot eyes and drooling mouth, thinking she might be the object of his affections.

When that stage of the tour was over, they were taken to spend a few days at a native African village.

The guide warned everybody not to step outside the compound. It could be dangerous. Rita woke sometime after midnight and went to wake her mother. Rattling the door knob produced no results. She need not have bothered the door was open and mam was gone. Rita paniced and went hollering for the security. The complex was searched. One Irish woman was missing. A search was mounted. No trace of missing mother. Someone suggested that she might have gone native. She had.

An hour or two later she was located in downtown 'No Man's Land.' Sitting around on the boardwalk outside the local drinking den was the missing miscreant shaking a tambourine with a motley crew of native musicians. Every time they finished a tune she regaled them with tall tales. They might have had no clue as to what she was saying, but the fact that a white woman had no fear of sitting down with them, added to the baboon bite on her arm, gave her a huge amount of street cred. She shared their home-brew in a jovial athmosphere, while the air hung heavy with the smell of gange.

'Hey mother! What the bloody hell are you doing here? Weren't you told this place was dangerous?'

Mam was wobbling from foot-to-foot. One step forward and two steps back. Some of her newly acquainted African entourage were performing the same steps. 'Rita,' The word came out slowly, in a slurred tone. 'I'm feeling funny.'

Between them, the security men carried her back to the complex.

Next morning Rita, who was not amused, decided to lay

down the law. The tirade of advice fell on deaf ears. When she finally ran out of puff, ma woke up.

'What's the matter with you Rita? I really don't know where I got you from girl. I had a great night. I saw the real Africa. These people aren't for the tourists. They're just like I am, piss poor. Church mice couldn't be any poorer. Lighten up girl. There's no harm in them. They come out at night, play a bit of music and sing a few songs. What's wrong with that?

Further more they really are poor. I saw it with my own eyes. They pool their tobacco and roll this one big cigarette. They pass it a from hand-to-hand and everyone has a puff. Much better than the stuff they sell at home. The tobacco in this place had a real kick. I felt I was floating.'

'Mother! You were stoned. That stuff might have killed you. What you were smoking was gange. Hemp, weed, cannabis, call it what you will, but you were having an out-of-body experience.'

'Oh! Was that what it was? When can I have another one?'

She came home and found a job in a local shop, Mr.Chickens where she quickly became a very popular member of staff. She used to cycle everywhere, never having learned to drive. On the front of her bike was a basket where her little pet Pekinese 'Snowball' loved to travel in style.

The next stop was some years later and eleven thousand miles from home. Where else, but in the land of sunshine and orange groves, California, on the west coast of America.

Rita had moved there and took mam out for a six month stay. As might be expected, she loved it. Living right on Long Beach, she was in her element. Blue skies, sun, sand, sea and surfers. This was a life-style she'd dreamed of and she lived it to the full.

Trouble was, a day came when she got itchy feet. She decided on a little exploring and ventured off the beaten track and out of the area she was slightly familiar with. She wandered on and in very few minutes was totally lost. She told me later, that as the day still young, the sun was shining and nowhere else to be, she'd thought she should do a bit of sightseeing. A woman on her own in downtown L.A.? Not an adventure to be recommended.

She walked on. Some time later she had a beer or two and the penny finally dropped. Outside of the fact that she was still in California, she'd absolutely no idea where she was, or how to contact Rita. This was in the pre-mobile phones era.

The sun, that previously had been pleasantly warm, was now a red ball of scorching, sweltering heat. Hell in a cloudless blue sky. Calling a taxi was an option, but she definitely didn't have enough for a fare. Getting to grips with dollars and cents was still a bridge too far, besides she'd heard tales of cab drivers. If they didn't get tipped, they'd run you over, or worse. She tried to think of a solution. Like pulling a lever on a slot machine, the cogs turned, all zeros. She wasn't hitting the jackpot. Nothing for it. Back to plan B, the old reliable. The rule of the thumb.

There was no hesitation or thinking involved. She marched over to the edge of the highway and stuck out her thumb. L.A. motorways are busy places. Cars, bumper to bumper and too many to count, along with dozens of trucks sped by. Trying to shield her eyes from the fireball in the sky, she almost missed the big gas guzzler that squealed to a stop right by her. The electric window slid down.

The sole occupant, an elderly man with a young man's head of hair and a thick moustach, said something in a language she didn't understand. He waved his hands about, all the time speaking at machine-gun speed. They understood each other. She wanted to travel, he was offering the ride. (No! It was all above board). It so happened the guy was from south of the border down Mexico way and had a fair spattering of English.

The address was on a slip of paper in her purse. Mexican Pedro knew the area. No bother to him. At the next set of mind-boggling flyovers, crossovers and underpasses, he reversed direction. Thirty minutes later he deposited her at Rita's front door. This was after first giving her a lecture on the doubtless stupidity of her actions.

'Senorita! You do not flag down strangers in L.A. It's a dangerous city. There are bad people here. It was a very stupid thing to do.' He went on to list all the possible outcomes there might have been to her escapade. Finally he drew his finger across his throat. The most pleasant ending was murder.

The luck of the Irish was with her that day.

A few years later she was back in California again. She was having a whale of a time. All credit to Rita who showed her everything she could. Mam loved nothing better than to gamble and going to the casinos of Las Vegas and Atlantic City were a total delight. She did actually hit the jackpot on a machine in Atlantic City and when coins started spilling out around the floor she could only stand there and scream. As she was only playing for small stakes it didn't amount to much (about $1700),but it certainly made her day.

When Rita took her to see the Kentucky Derby, it was certainly the biggest thrill she'd ever had in her life. Ma. loved horses with a total passion, and not just for the gambling aspect of it. She just loved horses. She brought me home a teeshirt from there that I still have to this day. It was that visit to the Bluegrass State of Kentucky that made her make a momentuos decision, which no one was aware of for many years.

Back in California, Rita came from work one day and found mother missing. Instant panic. She ran into the garden and found what she assumed was her lifeless body lying comatosed among the lettuces. She called the paramedics.

California being a hot weather state, the medical crew looked a little different to what she'd get at home. Mam was in a state for catching flies. Lying on her back, eyes closed and mouth wide open. These two West coast hunks were standing over her. Both over six feet, sun-tanned to bronze, wearing just skimpy shorts and sandles. All three were also equipped with six-packs. Yeah! These medics were serious workout merchants. Pulse checked, everything in order.

'Rita, does your mother like a beer, or maybe two?'

Problem solved. Mam had gone to an off-licence and bought herself a few too many Coors. She'd drank most of them and fell over in the vegetable patch. The medics hung around until she woke. First one eye opened. She stared unblinking at her saviors. After thirty seconds the other eye snapped open and had a peep. Then she sat bolt upright and screeched. 'Oh feck! I must have died and gone to heaven. Rita, this place is filled with angels.'

That was my mam alright. Always expect the unexpected. Even now, years later we laugh when we think of some of her exploits. The woman truly had a heart of gold and even though she's gone this twenty years, I still miss her.

After she came home the plans were laid for her to return and live in California permanently. I was going to buy her house, so she'd have enough money to give her some independance. Sadly due to unforseen circumstances, her plans had to be shelved.

From that day on her always cheerful disposition took a downward spiral. Even though she had great friends, (Every Saturday night, Connie left a naggin of whiskey in a bush ouside her front door. Danny always made sure the grass was cut and the garden kept neat and tidy.)

One cold Saturday morning, in early December, the lady from next door (a lifelong friend) found her lying on the sofa. Sometime in the night she'd passed away.

She'd often said she'd no wish to ever go into cold ground. The only crematorium at that time was in Dublin. It was what she wanted, and I'm so glad her wish was granted.

I cried so much that day I thought I'd never cry again. I was wrong. I'm crying now when I think of the biggest regret I ever had. I was touching fifty when she passed, and in all that time I never once did something that most people nowadays take for granted. I would love to have given my mother a hug and tell her how much I loved her. It never happened and I have to live with that. At times it's not easy.

A few weeks after the cremation, when the ashes were returned, was when I learned of her last request. She'd once asked Rita that when the time came, to see that her ashes were scattered on the famous Churchill Downs racecourse in Kentucky. It was done as requested.

She wanted to spend eternity resting on the ground by the winning post where the greatest horses in the world galloped. She got her wish.

Love you mam.

Just back from my daily walk in the woods. Beautiful morning. Sun shining. Nobody about. I sat on a fallen log enjoying the spectacular views, breathing the clean, sweet air. Just me and my shadows. What can one do in a place like that? Wishful thinking, meditation and contemplation perhaps. All the while living in hope. Making fantastic plans for a day that might never come.

My dogs were with me. Twister sat with his head on my knee and Buddy jumped onto my lap. There's love there and reassurance. I don't think I'm one deserving or worthy of such a morning, but I'll take it anyway. What did I do to be granted this amazing miracle of nature? I don't know.

I'm a failed Catholic and a well-flawed man, and yet today on the Ballyhoura Mountains in North Cork, I realised at ten minutes past eleven, that I'll probably never see Heaven, too much history between me and God, but I won't have to. You see, today, Heaven came to visit me.

Love y'all.

Lightning Source UK Ltd.
Milton Keynes UK
UKHW020639090221
378487UK00011B/325